ONLY YOU IN EVERYTHING

JENNIFER ANN SHORE

Print ISBN: 978-1-7360672-8-4

*For Carrie, a loyal reader, an incredible hype woman, and a
wonderful and supportive friend*

ONE

This, like many of the best things in life, is a total mess.

There's a thick layer of dust coating the disorganized space, and there's so much to do, I'm momentarily stuck trying to process what to tackle first.

I mentally catalog each and every square inch that needs my attention, then let out a breath, attempting to assuage my immediate panic.

But it doesn't work.

It definitely doesn't help that my expectation of this moment has been building for the past year, and my dreams are immediately dashed, along with the romantic notions I had for what would be waiting for me.

In my errant thoughts and thorough imagination, I pictured myself opening the door to find spotless counter-tops, meticulously arranged paintbrushes and bottles, and a view that, even after all these years, still makes my entire body feel at peace.

I should have known that wasn't my reality when the

planked wooden door refused to budge, and I had to leverage my body weight to force it open.

There's a throbbing pain where my upper arm meets my left shoulder, and I rub it with a grimace on my face, knowing an inevitable bruise will make an appearance within the next day or so.

The air is stale, weighing heavily and clouding my lungs, and I frown at the cobwebs that have taken up residence in every corner—along with what I can only assume is a mouse nest under the sink.

I give myself a few more comforting moments, letting the warm breeze do some of the legwork, before I drop my arm and the sour expression.

The shock eventually wears off—both from the sight before me and my necessarily violent entrance—and I begin the arduous task of readying the space for humans instead of animals, insects, filth, and possibly ghosts.

From the exterior, this little cabin is pretty unassuming.

It's a patchwork, rectangular structure of at least four different kinds of wood. Various slats and parts of the roof have been swapped who knows how many times, creating a sort of hodgepodge aesthetic that I find ridiculously charming.

The interior has a similar irregular vibe with a U-shaped table and mismatched chairs, and there's a counter covered in layers of long-dried paint that lines the back wall.

But my favorite part, aside from the tangible act of creating art within these walls, is the massive window overlooking the sprawling lake and the miles of trees that frame it.

To the untrained eye, this entire structure is almost

negligent, defiantly occupying an area that if left clear could provide awe-inducing views from the path.

I wholly disagree with that sentiment, though.

I'd even go as far as to say that there's no more fitting place on the grounds of Camp Creek to be designated for arts and crafts.

It takes a certain kind of person to appreciate the contrast and audacity of the structure for lasting this long. It's why I don't mind inhaling the dizzying combination of paint fumes and cleaning products, transforming this decrepit scene into something usable.

I fold a thick piece of paper in half a few times to wedge the door open, trying to circulate air. It doesn't offer much, so I plug in and turn on the fan that is definitely older than I am. I pound the back of it a few times to stop the clanging sound, then cough as the dust bunnies swirl off the blades.

My poor lungs can barely handle all the distress, so I put my hand on my chest until the coughs subside, even though I don't think my patience or light pressure makes a difference.

It would be such a shame to die of asphyxiation from rogue filth before the summer even really begins.

And I sincerely doubt the owners of the camp would be able to get another *unpaid* art director to fill my spot before the campers arrive on Saturday, so I suck it up and get to work.

Wiping the windows, dusting the counters, and sweeping the floor aren't my favorite summertime activities, but I lose myself in the process.

I always take a lot of pride in my space—whether it's my bedroom, car, or sketchbook—and the same goes for this cabin and program that I'll be responsible for in the next two months.

It feels like I've been waiting forever for this moment, and it's finally here.

I first arrived at Camp Creek as a camper the summer after second grade with Bellamy, my best friend, and Will, his twin brother. We played games and sang along to the radio as our mothers navigated the narrow roads up and around the mountains. When we finally arrived hours later, I was convinced this place was some sort of magical land enshrouded by trees.

And still, to this day, I haven't lost that sense of wonder.

Each summer brings a new mix of friends and additions to the property, but I've easily marked the years by the moments that stand out.

The year the owners, Rebecca and Matthew, updated their fleet of canoes was when Will really discovered his love for water sports—it also resulted in him spending three days in the health clinic after getting a second-degree sunburn.

Another summer, I had a brilliant idea to carve our names into a tree, only for it to be struck by lightning and catch on fire a month later. The blaze wasn't put out until after one of the storage sheds was reduced to ash. I tried not to take it as some sort of bad omen.

One year, Bellamy and I snuck out to pilfer food from the mess hall, only to take a detour through the woods riddled with poison ivy. We had to miss the overnight camping trip because our legs were covered with a terrible rash—which I wasn't totally heartbroken over—and it was the itchiest five days of my life.

This summer, however, we've vowed that it will be better than all the rest of the moments combined and then some.

Because this is *our* year.

We officially joined the volunteer staff of Camp Creek when we started high school, but now, after graduating and biding our time, it's all come together just how we hoped.

I get to run the arts program.

Bellamy leads the charge in the kitchen.

And Will...

I step up toward the now-clean window, getting an unobstructed view of him.

From my vantage point, he's no larger than my pointer finger, but I'd know that silhouette in a lineup of thousands.

As the leader of lakefront activities, he directs his team of volunteers to take the kayaks out of storage, likely reminding them all the best practices for care, as he shoves his mess of wavy black hair behind his ears.

I sigh in contentment, unaware of my own audience.

"Cameron," Bellamy says, tone light.

I turn, startled by the sound, to take in my best friend's amused expression.

I can't even pretend that I was doing anything practical because all the cleaning supplies are out of reach from where I'm standing.

"Hi," I return a little guiltily.

"If 'No, I can't hang out with you because I have to go get

the cabin ready' is just code for 'I'm going to shamelessly stare at Will for an extended period of time,' then I'm probably going to have to start saving you from yourself more often."

I don't bother to attempt to hide the blush that has definitely formed on my cheeks.

"You're lucky I find it endearing, not disgusting," Bellamy adds before hopping up on the counter.

"I just cleaned that," I huff.

"You have actually been productive, then?"

I narrow my eyes at him a little playfully before I gesture around us. "Can't you see?"

His gaze flickers around briefly before he gives me a pointed look and a shrug. "It really doesn't look that clean."

"Stop it," I chide, trying to hide my grin by snapping a rag at his calves.

"What?" Bellamy defends. "There's, like, twenty layers of paint right there."

I step over to the spot on the counter he's referencing to drag my fingertips over the specks and splashes of various colors.

"I think it's kind of pretty," I say. "I mean, you should consider all the projects and paintings made here. Not to mention the time spent at this very table. These are just little lasting remnants of creativity."

Bellamy chuckles softly. "Your ability to find beauty in anything is admirable, if not a little misguided."

I can't decide if he's right about that.

"How's it going in the mess hall?" I ask, pivoting topics.

"Great," he says proudly. "All organized and already started on prep for the weekend."

"Lucky you," I say without an ounce of annoyance.

"Well, I have a whole team to coordinate, and you just have the brushes and sponges to keep you company." He runs a hand over his buzzed hair as he glances upward. "And this creepy mural."

I don't bother looking upward.

Because the black and white painting of flowers and angels, which takes up the entire ceiling, is permanently etched into my brain.

"It's not creepy," I argue for probably the hundredth time in our lives. "It's beautiful."

"I don't see it." Bellamy shakes his head as he pushes his sleeves up, revealing the tattooed roses all up his forearm. "But I trust your judgment. Obviously. I mean, who else could I go along with if not the person who spent all spring break trying to create the perfect shade of green?"

Before me now are at least a dozen different bottles of that very color, though dust obscures the names on the labels.

I cross my arms over my chest. "It's still a work in progress."

Bellamy looks longingly at all the paint containers that still need tending to. "Aren't we all?"

"So you came by to help, then?" I tease.

He hops off the ledge, landing easily on his feet. "Hell no."

I mentally curse him for being so coordinated and suave all the time.

"I'm just on my way down to the clinic," he says.

I exaggerate a pout. "Did you strain yourself by ordering people around all morning?"

He grins and shakes his head. "It's vitamin T time."

His words are casual, but even after six months of hormone therapy, we're still both ecstatic and in slight disbelief that he's able to get it.

Bellamy transitioned socially a few years ago, but after years of therapy and long conversations with his parents, he began taking testosterone when he turned eighteen.

His weekly shot—which we've affectionately named vitamin T—helps him continue to outwardly match who he's always been inside.

"Kind of sucks that you can't just do it yourself like you have been this whole time," I say with a sigh.

"I don't mind," he admits honestly. "They have the good lollipops this year, and I've already scoped out all the different bandages I get to choose from."

I laugh at his excitement. "I'll have to get you a variety pack for Christmas, then. I didn't realize that was an important part of the process."

"Real men wear Batman Band-Aids," Bellamy says with a smile as he walks toward the door. "Come by the mess hall when you're done here, okay? I think I'm going to make a batch of brownies in a bit."

"Peanut butter brownies?" I say, my mouth watering at the thought. "With extra chocolate chips on top?"

"I don't think the Camp Creek budget has accounted for your sweet tooth."

I roll my eyes even though he's not wrong. "Get out of here before I put you to work."

"Terrifying." He mock-shudders before he retreats.

I hold onto the joy for just a little while longer, then eventually renew my focus on the tasks I abandoned for the staring and conversing. I finish up the general cleaning before finding a working pen among all the supplies and jotting down what we need to add to the inventory.

Last spring, when I was officially offered the position for the summer, I asked Rebecca and Matthew for a few supplies off the top of my head.

I knew we'd need additional palettes and pre-formed canvases for some of the older kids, but the younger ones will mostly be painting pictures on the scrap wood and thick paper that seems to be spawning in every corner.

I scribble down a few things—kneaded erasers, more basic acrylic white paint, a new pack of scissors with those different shaped blades—then admire my own blocky handwriting.

A delighted scream from the water below brings me back to the window, and I cross the space once again to watch the group laugh and splash around.

I smile, watching Will's long and lean body move with relaxed ease.

Seeing him act carefree without the burdens of our past and present does something to my heart and soul that I try very hard to not let myself succumb to.

But it's in these stolen glances where he's unaware of his surroundings and my appreciation for him that I can't help but fall for him all over again.

Almost as if he senses my thoughts, he tilts his head up in the direction of the cabin.

I back away from the glass immediately as my mind runs wild with false ideas that he's caught me spying on him. With that mortifying line of thinking spurring me on,

I grab my list and head out, finally leaving my now-clean sanctuary.

As I head up toward the mess hall, I can't decide what brings about a greater feeling of euphoria—Bellamy's peanut butter brownies or the sight of Will in a moment of unfettered happiness.

TWO

Before I met Will and Bellamy, my upbringing was normal by most people's standards—brick house, fence in the front yard, family dinner on Sundays, that sort of thing.

I remember somewhat blurry moments with my sister, Piper, and our parents, who raised two mild-mannered girls who favored frilly dresses, overly large bows in their hair, and were perfectly content spending the afternoon playing with dolls.

The day the Moreno family's massive moving truck rolled onto our street made the quiet summer afternoon somehow seem ridiculously loud. It wasn't the volume of the music blasting on the radio from the moving truck or sounds of exertion in unloading their furniture—it was the disruption of my life as I knew it.

My mother, with a welcome gift of store-bought banana bread and a list of nearby restaurants and shops in hand, led Piper and me across the street to greet them.

It took all of three minutes for Will and Bellamy to drag

me out into their wooded backyard and indoctrinate me into their antics, and I was immediately hooked.

The first time I came home with muddied tennis shoes and a request for more practical clothing—no more tulle, especially—my mother was concerned.

I wasn't exactly all-in on the running around all the time and playing games in the big pile of leaves and dirt at the edge of their property, but the twins were so hyperactive that it was bound to rub off on me.

I think she and my dad thought Will and Bellamy would outrun me at some point and never look back, but it never happened.

Instead, I became a mainstay on their many adventures and a regular at their dinner table. It was our friendship that brought our families close, and it's been that way ever since, resulting in years of shared parties, weekend trips, and movie nights.

And yet out of all the framed pictures and fond memories, it's the recollection of one impromptu bike ride that's most visceral, even today.

It was an early autumn Saturday just like any other.

The leaves already started to change colors, encouraged by the little chill in the air that my favorite bubblegum pink sweatshirt protected me from.

Our parents were busy watching some baseball game, an activity that Elena—Bellamy and Will's mom—coaxed my parents into joining in on over time.

My sister was at some friend's house, but the remaining offspring, the three of us, decided to go outside and deface our newly paved street.

We drew hopscotch and those crime-scene inspired

outlines of one another in chalk, which almost served as eerie premonition of what was to come, then Bellamy suggested we race down the street.

Without a bike of my own, I got relegated to being pedaled along on Will's handlebars.

I didn't mind it all that much because, even though the metal line wasn't a comfortable seat, my precarious position made it perfectly reasonable for me to lean back against his chest for support.

Even then, I was so hopelessly in love with him that the instant we made contact, I swear all sorts of nerve endings burst, creating a stuttering of my heart while we zoomed along. I've never once been electrocuted, but I imagine that's what it would feel like.

We cruised at high speed, testing the limits of his Schwinn, and a laugh of elation escaped from my mouth as the rumble roared in his chest, a sign of his own enjoyment.

I couldn't help what came next because I was selfishly and physically compelled to see his reaction for myself. At the time, I didn't understand the feelings behind that impulse, but after almost ten years of thinking about it every single day, I get it now.

I twisted back slightly to catch a glimpse of him, needing to take in the brilliant grin on his features and the fun and lightness encapsulated within it.

The wind whooshed by us as we sped along, and my eyes locked with his.

It was *just* enough of a distraction that neither of us were looking ahead to see the car turning right into us.

One second I was smiling and reveling in the wind, and

the next I was one with the air before I landed facedown with a thud. I hit the concrete sidewalk instead of that freshly dried black road, and the rough material scraped my delicate skin through the holes in my jeans.

Even now, with so many years and therapy sessions passed, I can still smell the rubbery, burnt scent of fresh asphalt just as viscerally as I can hear Bellamy's screams.

I don't think any amount of time or talking through the guilt will make me forget the screech of tires as the car drove off or the sight of Will's body lying twisted at an unnatural angle.

Will had to spend a month in the hospital recovering from the force of the impact. He underwent multiple surgeries to repair his broken hip and leg, but he'd have lasting nerve damage for the rest of his life.

Along with that, the massive and very jagged cut along his face would leave him scarred permanently.

Much like the ordeal itself.

I got off easy, walking away with three fractured fingers, a broken wrist, and bruised ribs.

My biggest challenge was settling on what cast color I wanted—bright orange, the shade of the summer sun I missed so desperately—while he had to learn how to *walk* again with the help of Bellamy, his parents, and a team of doctors and physical therapists.

Our friendship faltered, and, much like the accident, it was all my fault.

I was too young to process the event and repercussions fully, and as a result, I was a constantly moving seesaw of emotions.

I'd spend weekends zoned out in front of the television,

not even really watching anything or eating whatever meals my parents placed in front of me, then get a renewed sense of valiancy and determination that I could singlehandedly fix everything.

I'd show up to see Will—at first in the hospital then in his bedroom—with the best intentions, only to immediately break down into loud, full body sobs that served as an outlet for the guilt.

After maybe the dozenth time of this, Bellamy approached me after school one day to say that Will needed a break from me, which marked the first, last, and only time that Bellamy would ever take sides between his brother and his best friend.

And just like that, the three of us stopped being *us*.

I sat alone on the bus and at school, secluding myself from my usual lunch table and our mutual friends as continued self inflicted punishment, and it only got worse when Will eventually came back to school.

It was, without a doubt, the worst feeling in the world to watch them live their lives without me in it.

It wasn't until that following summer at Camp Creek that we came back together. The change in scenery and the general elation of being at our favorite place in the world put us right back where we once were—with a few notable changes.

Will had always loved the water, but that summer was when he really got into it. Kayaking, canoeing, sailing, and all those other activities were the only ones offered at Camp Creek that didn't tire out his still-recovering leg too quickly.

Bellamy approached me, the only interaction between

us I'd ever noted him to be anything close to sheepish, and asked me to cut off his waist-length hair.

And I started drawing.

It was just a little exercise, suggested by my own medical staff, to find something low impact to help recover my wrist's dexterity.

My parents didn't hate the idea of an activity to keep my eight-year-old self occupied for hours at a time, so they sent me a box of pencils and a drawing pad of my very own to supplement what the seldom-used art cabin offered.

While the others were running around in the sunshine, I drew.

I started with Will's scar, then added to it, creating little triangles in a zigzag formation—using it as the backdrop served as a blank canvas to spur my imagination forward.

I turned the lines into ice cream cones, mountains, pizza slices, and whatever else came to mind. Then I did the same with circles, creating the sun and chocolate chip cookies and baseballs until my wrist and fingers were too stiff to hold a pencil any longer.

I've definitely evolved from that practice, expanding mediums and creating more complex pieces.

But as a starting point, an ode to where my talent began, I always incorporate the serrated line I'm responsible for on Will's features.

My art teacher called it my signature, claiming it's more notable than my tiny signature scrawled in the corner.

Unless you know to look for it, though, you won't even know it's there.

I, of course, pick up on it everywhere, even outside of

my work—I see that jagged mark in constellations, rivers, stretches of highway, and even the stems of flowers.

And I glance at it now as Will enters the camp's mess hall.

He's flanked by his volunteers, and he laughs at something one of them says before giving his full attention to Bellamy, who is standing behind the counter.

I watch fondly as they chat for a moment, undoubtedly telling each other about whatever they've been up to since breakfast.

Bellamy slides Will's tray toward him, then he pulls it back just before he's able to grasp it. The near miss causes Bellamy to roar with laughter, but Will rolls his eyes and says something to him I can't catch.

Whatever it is, though, it causes Bellamy to point toward me, and I blink as Will turns to smile at me, then finally grabs his food and heads toward me.

I take a sip of Camp Creek's famous bug juice—which Bellamy informed me is just watered-down Kool-Aid—and try to act nonchalant as Will walks over.

Despite the horsing around he did earlier, he's walking without issue, and I'm instantly relieved at the sight of it.

One of the lasting consequences of the accident is that Will's limp becomes more pronounced when he overexerts himself, something that I've found myself embarrassingly attuned to over the years.

In school, he had a blanket doctor's note to get out of all physical activity, but he stubbornly insisted on doing the mile run last year. I don't think I've seen him have a more difficult time downplaying his struggle.

He's almost always too proud to admit he's in pain, but

I can always sense and see it—the stiffness in his stride, the deepening lines around his eyes, the way his mouth tightens.

But now, thankfully, he's all light and airy, radiating happiness.

He takes the seat beside me and lets his tray clang on the table. "Are my nostrils deceiving me, or is that—"

"Bellamy's peanut butter brownies," I finish for him. "Yep."

"Your doing, I assume?" Will asks before taking a bite of his sandwich.

"Maybe," I return coyly. "There aren't extra chocolate chips, though."

The corner of his mouth ticks up as he shakes his head. "The audacity of him."

I can't withhold my grin. "How dare he, right? Thinking he can make them without the most crucial topping."

"What will we do with him?" Will says, exasperated. "You know, I've been trying to talk Bellamy into becoming a pastry chef instead of pursuing his Wall Street dream."

"Wait, me too," I admit seriously as I stab my little portion of salad with a fork. "Why he is sold on studying *finance* of all things, I'll never understand. Especially because he's the worst of the three of us at saving money."

"Well, maybe studying this will help him," Will suggests before helping himself to a large swig from my glass. "How'd it go in the cabin, by the way? I stopped by on the way up here, but you were already gone."

I sink my teeth into my bottom lip, reminding myself not to outwardly react to something that seems oddly intimate.

Like how his mouth was just where mine was…

I brush that off because I know now it's just contentment and years of being around one another that has removed some layers of boundaries between us.

But I can't help the general sense of belonging I feel around him or the way his little nonchalant admissions make me feel all warm and fidgety.

I wish things were different, but Will made it clear last summer that he doesn't *like me* in that way.

It was here, at this very camp, that I tried to tell him I wanted more than friendship with him, and he shut me down before I could even finish stumbling through my declaration.

It was hard for me to process, and in some ways, I still am working through it.

The longing is clear on my end in every moment we spend together because he's so thoughtful and wonderful—I mean, he once told me how much he hates when we go a few days without spending time together.

It'd take an alien or some sort of saint to be able to withstand that sentiment, and I'm neither of those things.

"The cabin is good," I eventually answer. "I got everything cleaned and organized. But I need a few other things."

Will glances up, completely disarming me with his soft gaze. "Anything I can help with?"

I take a sip of juice, putting my lips right over the spot his just were. Because, apparently, I'm a glutton for punishment who also leans heavily toward psychopathic behavior.

"Do you happen to have an industrial-sized vat of Mod

Podge anywhere?" I ask him, keeping my voice as even as I can.

"No," Will answers with a laugh. "I'm only in possession of a sailboat that's on the brink of death, with a massive hole in the hull, and a few life vests that need to be sewn back together."

"I'll keep that in mind," I say, biting back a smile.

"Welcome, welcome, counselors, crew, and directors," the familiar, slightly high-pitched voice calls for all of our attention.

"Here we go," Will says before we both turn toward the middle of the cluster of tables.

Rebecca steps up on a bench to continue addressing everyone. "Camp Creek has missed you during the off-season, and we're so happy to see so many familiar faces back here. And that's even *before* all our campers arrive on Saturday!"

Matthew cups his hands around his mouth in an attempt to amplify his voice. "Before you finish up your meals and wander off for the afternoon, we do have a few announcements."

Rebecca nods. "First order of business, the new programs this year are as follows..."

I should be listening, but instead, I'm staring at Will's profile.

Even in all the time we spend together, it's rare I get a totally unobstructed view of his right side.

He normally attempts to cover it with his hair or cups his cheek to mask it with his hand, and I suppose it's an honor that he's relaxed enough in my presence that it's not a concern.

I take in the scar that I've drawn and painted an incalculable number of times.

It starts just above his eyebrow and cuts down across his cheekbone, ending just before it hits the top of his lip. It's usually the first thing anyone notices when they meet him.

But I see so much more than that.

Like when his brow furrows in concentration because he's *really* listening to Rebecca's rambling.

And the way he dabs his mouth with his napkin three times because he misses the little spot of mustard on the first two tries.

And how when he smiles, it takes him two attempts, like his mouth needs to test out the expression before it can come to fruition.

I love every single one of those things about him.

I'm still studying him when he tilts his head, rolling out his neck, and I quickly refocus my attention back on Rebecca—apparently just in time.

"Cameron," she calls, scanning the room.

"Yes?" I reply.

She grins as she finally finds me among the tables. "Yes, hi. I got the list of materials you left on my desk. Thank you. We'll take care of those as soon as we can, but I did want to let you know your roommate will be here shortly. Tori, the head of the soccer program I mentioned."

I hide my frown at the news that I won't have a space all to myself, but I try my best to seem pleased.

"Great," I say, mustering as much enthusiasm as I can. "Thank you."

As she moves on to the next item on the checklist, I lean over just slightly toward Will.

"We have a soccer program?" I whisper.

"It's new." He shakes his head, but I catch the amusement on his features. "Where have you been for the past ten minutes?"

I shrug before I take a massive bite of food.

It is a valid question, but it's one I'm definitely not going to answer.

THREE

Within the culture of camp employees, there's an unspoken line of demarcation between the counselors and the crew.

Although we're "all on the same team," according to Rebecca, there's clear resentment, and it's completely one-sided.

It's because we crew members have our own quarters separated from the campers, while the counselors have to share bunk beds and bathroom space with kids all under the age of thirteen.

As far as I'm concerned, that's their choice.

I barely tolerated sharing a space with twelve other girls my age when I was one of them, and there was no way in hell I was going to come back here to relive that as I got older, so I always volunteered specifically for crew services.

The others could have done the same, but they opted for that role and those accommodations.

It's not like the little crew cabins are glamorous—even though Bellamy and Will joked all winter in exaggerated pretentious voices about how excited they were to get back to their "summer home."

As I relax in my glorified shack, I appreciate that even though it's simple, it's private. There are two twin beds, one set of shared shelves, and a tiny bathroom where the shower, sink, and toilet are practically all on top of each other.

My roommate last year was overly chatty and very much in my business, driving me away.

I'm not sure if that was a tactical move on her part to have the space to herself, but I spent most of my spare time in the mess hall, bothering Bellamy as he worked shifts as a dishwasher.

It seems this time around, I'm going to be rooming with a real-life sporty Barbie.

"Hi," she says as she enters, dropping her two massive duffel bags on the floor. "I'm Tori."

I pause my music and set aside my sketchbook, then shake her extended hand. "Cameron."

"Oh my gosh, what happened?" Tori asks, voice full of concern as she turns my hands over. "Nevermind."

She releases my grasp, and I look at my fingers, which are covered with smudged graphite on one side.

"I've been drawing all afternoon," I explain, gesturing to my bedspread. "But I guess it does kind of look like a bruise."

"I'm sure I'll come back here with plenty of bumps and *actual* bruises this summer," she says proudly.

I blink in confusion, unsure of why that's something to boast about. "Oh."

"Was that a little douchey?" Tori asks with a wince.

I laugh nervously. "Um, not—"

"I'm not, like, happy about injuring myself. It's just part of the job. I'm trying to work on my aggression off the field, but if you're tough, you're tough. Anyway..." She puts her hands on her hips and surveys her portion of our lodgings. "This is mine, then? And these shelves?"

"Yeah. I was going to apologize for leaving you the top shelves, but I don't think I'll need to now."

Tori smiles and makes a show of stretching her long and tanned legs. "But now that you see I'm nearly six feet tall, you're fine with it?"

"Pretty much," I say with a small smile.

She drops down and starts unpacking, pulling out piles of knee socks and athletic shorts—two items I've never worn a day in my life.

"Is that Joy Division?" Tori asks me, appraising my wardrobe choices while I do the same to her.

I glance down at the slightly wrinkled shirt that I haphazardly shoved on this morning, along with ripped jean shorts that have a few blobs of green paint on them.

"Yeah," I say, averting my eyes from my appearance. "You like that band?"

"Not really," she admits casually. "I like more upbeat music. You know, the kind of stuff you can dance and sing along to."

"I don't blame you," I tell her. "I'm just a little picky about what I listen to when I'm drawing or painting. I find that alternative and indie and a lot of music from the eighties and nineties fits my brain."

"That makes sense. I do the same thing. I *have* to listen to really powerful stuff when I run. It helps me push on when all I want to do is give up." She rifles through her bag with determination. "Yes! See?"

She holds up a shirt with an absolutely stunning depiction of Lizzo naked.

I think the original image is from one of her album covers, but this one looks like a fan went in and redrew it, adding flowers and cursive letters around her form.

I smile at the sight of it. "Well, of course. Even I can appreciate Lizzo."

"I think we're going to get along just fine," Tori says genuinely.

Before I can respond, she strips off her plain shirt in favor of the one she just showed me, then makes a big show of brushing off her hands.

I don't think I'm too modest of a person, but I'm jealous at the way she doesn't give a second thought at being so exposed to someone she just met.

I can't decide if it's an athlete thing or simple confidence.

"I'm bored of unpacking," Tori says a little flippantly. "Want to go do something?"

I note that she managed to get only a fraction of her belongings out of her bag.

But I'm not going to judge if she'd rather spend her first few minutes at Camp Creek outside of our cramped space.

"How about a tour of the property?" I offer.

"That'd be great," she says excitedly. "I checked out the map on the way here. But seeing more of the place for myself would be awesome."

I jump up and slide on my sandals, then lead the way out the screen door. "I'm happy to. Let's head up this way."

"What were you drawing?" Tori asks after a few steps.

"Nothing in particular," I lie easily enough.

I'm trying to convince both her and myself that it's no big deal, that my drawing is some errant hobby.

The truth is that I feel tremendous pressure at the moment because the deadline looms for a prestigious fall internship I'm desperate to land.

I'm trying to distract myself from pining over Will and my nerves at creating something worthy of impressing an actual artist, but I've pretty much hemorrhaged my emotions in a way that has stunted my creativity.

I haven't liked anything I've created in paint, charcoal, pencil—hell, I even tried using a crayon last week, and the sketch still went in the garbage.

"It didn't look like nothing," she presses.

I ignore that insinuation and smile brightly as we come to a crossroads.

Literally.

And a little metaphorically.

"So, down this path is all the crew space, and up here, we'll walk toward the middle of Camp Creek," I say, turning away to gesture to the surroundings. "If you ever get lost, just try to get to the mess hall, and you should be able to find your way from there."

Her eyes are slightly narrowed at my evasion, but thankfully, she stays on target. "I passed the soccer field on the way here."

"Then you've also seen the climbing wall and the basketball court?" I ask her, piecing together what she's missing.

"Uh-huh."

"How about the pool?"

She shakes her head. "I must have missed that."

"Got it," I say, planning the best route for us to take. "Follow me."

Tori does so without complaint, making commentary about activities and some of her past experiences with camps and soccer practices while we walk.

If I had a blank piece of paper and the topography of Camp Creek, I'm completely certain I wouldn't have designed it this way.

The truth is that while over the years the property has added some pretty cool amenities for campers, it's pretty spread out and slightly illogical.

For example, the pool is nearly on the opposite side of the property from the lake, which means campers run through the main path getting dirt stuck to their feet and getting their towels soggy before they're done with water activities for the day.

Also, the climbing wall, which is a massive rectangular structure with climbing holds on all four sizes is in the middle of the gravel parking lot. I assume because it had already been level ground when they went to install it.

But it's a little odd that a seven-year-old's best view from that height is of my old Ford Explorer.

Poor organization aside, it pretty much only takes a few steps in any direction to appreciate the beauty and fresh-ness of being in "nature"—or as close to it as I'm comfort-able with being.

I'm not surprised by my own enthusiasm as I show Tori around, even introducing her to some of the other crew members along the way.

She flawlessly navigates each social interaction with ease, making jokes and immediately connecting with our peers.

"This place is more gorgeous than I imagined," Tori gushes as she and I walk toward the mess hall.

I can't help but smile at that declaration.

Her appreciation for a place I love so much warms me to her even more.

"It's pretty great," I say as I open the door.

"And you've been coming here forever," Tori says. "I'm pretty jealous, honestly. This is a huge upgrade from that place in Arizona my parents shipped me off to last summer."

"What was wrong with that one?" I ask.

She shudders at whatever memory is in her head. "Just imagine running eight miles a day in the desert heat and sun."

I wrinkle my nose at that thought.

"Exactly," Tori says, nodding to the expression on my face. "Three months summarized by one grimace."

"Well, hopefully this one is far better for you."

She smiles. "Me too."

We grab our trays of chicken parmesan from one of Bellamy's kitchen minions, who Tori winks at, then I lead her over to my usual table.

She glances around to check out the other counselors and crew members before she takes the seat across from me, eyes now glued to the sight of the delicious dinner before us.

I don't know if this dinner was already planned or if Bellamy specifically chose this because it's my favorite meal of all time, but whatever the reason, I'm elated to use the side of my fork like a knife and dig in.

It's melty and savory with the cheese yet somehow crisp with breading, garlic, and pepper.

And it's absolutely amazing.

"Oh, damn," Tori says, covering her mouth to let out those words.

I swallow my bite. "Right? Insanely good."

"I'm going to eat my way through this summer, and I love this for me," she says before diving in for another forkful.

We're too focused on our plates to hold a conversation, and I'm just fine with that.

This is one of the remaining semi-quiet meals I'll have this summer in the mess hall. I can appreciate each bite without worrying about some prank unfurling at one of the camper tables or sudden shriek from a group of eight-year-old girls.

"Who is *that?*" Tori asks suddenly, breaking through the silence.

I glance up to see her utensil hovering as she practically drools over whoever she's looking at, then I follow her eyes.

A panicky sort of pounding hits my chest as I take in Will sauntering across the mess hall, then watch in horror as he offers a fist bump to Bellamy over the counter.

Even from this distance, I can tell they're speaking rapidly in Spanish—as they often do at home with their parents—much to the annoyance of the kitchen volunteers who are clearly trying to eavesdrop.

Bellamy rolls his eyes at whatever is making Will laugh

before he adds an extra helping of chicken parmesan to his tray.

I tear my eyes away, looking back to Tori as Will approaches, only to have ten thousand pounds of weight lifted from my body as I realize her gaze remains fixed behind him.

And right on Bellamy.

The relief is instantaneous.

And I'm also a little giddy by this change of events.

"That's my best friend," I tell her proudly. "It's *his* chicken parm recipe you're eating."

"Even better," she says, a little smug. "Name?"

"Bellamy Moreno."

A devilish grin appears on her features. "That's the coolest name I've ever heard. Like, rockstar sexy, you know?"

I laugh, not entirely disagreeing. "Bellamy's parents are Cuban, but one of their ancestors was French, which is where I think his first name came from."

"Ooh," Tori breathes before finally taking and quickly swallowing her bite. "So, what's his deal? Is he single? Is he cool? What's he into?"

"Who is what now?" Will asks as he sits down beside me.

I smile at his question, but Tori only gives him a brief glance before she turns back to Bellamy.

"Him," Tori tells Will as she shamelessly points directly at Bellamy.

Will raises an eyebrow, amused expression clear on his features. "That's my brother."

"And this is Will," I offer, waving my fork in his direction. "They're twins."

She turns and squints at him, clearly checking out the resemblance.

They're fraternal, so while their features and builds are similar, the differences are clear—even when not taking into account Will's distinguishing scar.

Bellamy's hair is faded on the sides and cut close up top, while Will's is a shoulder-length, tangled mess. Will is a "I'll wear whatever's within reach" kind of guy, but Bellamy takes tremendous care in his appearance, even going as far as ironing his t-shirts, which Will and I have teased him for, and is obsessed with collecting and wearing old-school basketball shoes.

"So, which one of you is going to introduce me?" Tori asks, finally giving us her full attention once again. "Actually, scratch that, I'll just figure out a way to do it myself."

I laugh and shake my head. "This is Tori," I say for Will's benefit.

"Figured that," Will says, pushing the extra plate of dinner toward me. "This is for you, by the way. Figured you could use some more of your favorite."

My face nearly splits in half at the gesture. "Thank you."

"You're welcome," he says before he swipes my juice.

Tori's gaze flicks between us, assessing the dynamic, before she lets out a sigh. "So, what's there to do around here, aside from the, like, camp-y stuff?"

"Well, we really only get Saturdays off," Will explains. "And even then, we usually have to rotate in on supervising shifts."

"Right, but like, we don't have anything scheduled tonight," Tori ventures. "So what's the plan?"

"The plan?" I echo.

"Well, you don't expect me to sit around and fondle my thumbs all night, do you?" Her tone is completely exasperated.

Will blinks. "Oh, uh, no?"

"I'm going to get another serving," she announces, then abruptly stands.

I watch, equal parts confused and impressed as she sashays up toward the counter, grinning at Bellamy as she approaches.

I open my mouth, close it, then open it again. "Did she just say—"

"I think it's—" Will shakes his head. "'Twiddle' is a strange word, I guess."

"But *fondle*?" I repeat.

We both fall into quiet laughter, and it makes me wonder how many more of these little moments we'll share here this summer.

FOUR

"It's Friday night, baby!" Tori announces as she flings open the flimsy bathroom door.

"I know," I say with slight irritation because it's the eighth time she has made this declaration.

I still smile, though, and it's reflected back at me in the mirror I'm holding aloft to inspect my lipstick.

"I've been waiting for this all week," she says.

I chuckle at her enthusiasm. "Tori, you've been here for three days, and the campers haven't even arrived yet."

And in that time, I've learned that Tori is what can be described as a human who only functions at the highest of speeds.

She likes to have every waking hour filled with movement, whether it's eating, playing cards in the floor of our cabin, going for runs, or organizing her equipment.

It's productive, certainly, but it also means she leaves a tornado in her wake—in this current case, it's every single piece of clothing she owns not on her designated shelving.

"So?" Tori fires back as she whips off her towel.

I sigh and quickly avert my eyes.

Because another one of her delightful traits I've picked up on so far is that modesty isn't a thing around her, which is slowly becoming less jarring with each passing outfit change.

Despite all that and her changes to common idioms, she's forceful, brilliant, and well spoken, especially when she's trying to get things done her way.

And I, honestly, am totally charmed by her.

"That's even better," Tori continues, finishing her perusal and turning back to me. "A last blast of fun before the real work starts."

"I just don't even know how you heard of this place we're going to," I mutter.

I concentrate on making sure my drawn-on cat eye is even, but I can see her quick movement in my peripheral vision.

"One of the counselors told me," she says as she zips her jean shorts. "I think she's from cabin ten?"

I glance up at her, mouth agape in shock. "Wait, what?" I sputter. "You're friends with the enemy?"

She scoffs while tugging on her tank top. "I'm friends with everyone. Don't worry, though. You're still special, Cameron."

"I wasn't worried," I tell her honestly.

She tosses her crumpled towel aside and smiles as she sits on my bed, then tilts her head toward my cosmetic bag. "Will you do that to me?"

"Sure," I agree. "But you're going to have to hold still."

"Fine," she breathes.

I study her for a beat, trying to decide what to do.

Tori is classically pretty in the typical all-American kind of way—symmetrical features, bright blue eyes, perfectly formed full lips—and she only needs the lightest layers of emphasis.

I pull out three options of foundation, then mix them on the back of my hand in an attempt to match her perfectly tanned-by-the-sun complexion.

"There's a very sacred divide between us and the counselors," I tell her as I work. "Built upon years of distant hatred and jealousy."

"And I've dismantled it within just a few days," Tori says smartly. "In the spirit of unity, go me."

I chuckle as I start to blend my creation on her face with a sponge. "Congratulations."

She forces her smile to dissipate as I do my thing, holding as still as I've ever seen her.

I take my time contouring her cheekbones just enough to highlight the severity of the lines, then I abandon my tools to hand-blend a light shade of pink for her blush, just enough to make the color pop.

As I adjust her eyeliner for the fifth time, she starts getting antsy, hands and feet twitching in anticipation of leaving.

"How much longer is this going to take?" Tori asks, tapping my thigh impatiently.

I frown at my selection of eyeshadow palettes. "I'm not sure. I've never done anyone else's makeup before."

"Cameron," she whines as I attempt to smudge the colors on her lids. "We have to leave in, like, ten minutes."

"I know."

"You're a freaking *artist*. I mean, I've never seen a steadier hand with a brush or more care into creating the shadows of trees or whatever."

"Are you just saying that because you want something from me?" I tease as I pull back, nodding in satisfaction.

"No, but who cares if I was?" Tori asks, closing her eyes once again. "But maybe speed is our friend in this case. And red lipstick."

"Fine," I relent, unable to hide my smile as I finish my work. "We're done."

I hand over the mirror, and Tori's eyes bug out at the sight.

"Oh my gosh, Cameron," she says excitedly. "This is... wow! How did you do this? I once got my makeup professionally done for my cousin's wedding, and I looked like a clown. But this is incredible. The colors, the blending, the everything, it's—"

"Shouldn't we head out?" I ask with a smirk.

"Yes, yes," she says.

But she's almost reluctant to put down the mirror.

As we walk to my car, the compliments continue, and Tori goes on and on about my talent and how good she looks.

The only time she pauses during the ride is to admire herself in her front-facing camera, leaving me to fend for myself on figuring out how to get to our destination.

Being in the middle of the mountains of Pennsylvania doesn't exactly make anywhere around Camp Creek a hotbed for nightlife.

I think the most exciting off-property plans I've had since

joining the crew was doing a convenience store run with Will —or the time Bellamy insisted on finding a dry cleaner when one of his favorite shorts got stained with tomato sauce.

But, as Tori informs me, there's a "bar *slash* restaurant" that stays open late every Friday, and it's here that the counselors have opted to have their one last blast to celebrate the final night of freedom before camp starts.

"Oh my gosh, there's karaoke," Tori gushes, leading me through the threshold with her arm wrapped around mine. "This is so cool."

I'm not exactly impressed, though.

I glance around at the stained walls, scratched wooden countertops, and dark floors that are more scuffed than polished.

"'Cool' is a bit of a reach," I say on an exhale.

Tori rolls her eyes as she tugs me through the crowd. "Don't be such a snob."

"I'm not," I argue while sidestepping a burly man chugging beer from a glass the size of my head. "I just...don't think we should eat or drink anything here."

"Brody snuck in alcohol, anyway," Tori says proudly. "I'll just get some cans of pop and mix them in the bathroom."

If this area is dirty, I can't imagine how the bathrooms are faring.

"I'll pass."

"Oh, come on," Tori chides me. "Lighten up."

"I have to drive," I remind her.

"Fine," she breathes before plastering on a big smile as we reach the group. "Brody, Caitlin, hey!"

The two counselors greet her with enthusiasm, then offer me polite waves, which I return easily.

They've been dating for at least the past two summers, if my memory is correct, and I've always thought they were a really cute pairing. Brody is a hulking bear of a human, making even Tori look small in comparison, and he's got hair longer than mine and thicker than Will's. Caitlin has a wide smile and a double nose piercing, and her style is somehow simultaneously chic and laid-back.

I watch Tori take charge in getting everyone to drink and name their go-to karaoke song, while I hang back, watching all the commentary and sipping on the Sprite that Caitlin kindly orders for me.

Tori's the life of the party, and I'm in no way surprised by this.

This, quite clearly, is not my scene, but then again, I'm not sure what *is*.

With the exception of my own family and the Morenos, I can't think of a crowd of people I've ever been comfortable in. It's not an attention issue, though, because I've never faltered while giving presentations in school or putting my art on display.

But somehow, opening up to strangers in a social setting seems daunting.

I'd much prefer to stand back and watch it all happen, staying connected without actively participating—observing, not judging. Well, maybe a little bit of the latter because I can't help but cringe as Tori takes a large swig from Brody's flask.

They all take turns sipping and sharing funny stories

from previous summers at camp, and as the minutes go by, I guess I see why this experience is such a bonding one.

"Don't you think it's a little strange that all of these people are going to be responsible for children as of tomorrow morning?"

At first, I wonder if my own inner monologue has morphed into Will's voice.

But when he slides onto the barstool next to mine, I can't stop the embarrassing grin from forming on my face.

"I mean, who knows where that flask has been?" Will jokes.

"The better question," Bellamy ventures, hovering behind me, "is how can I get my hands on it?"

"I thought you guys weren't coming," I accuse, bringing Bellamy down for a hug.

Bellamy snorts. "Mom was actually pissed that we were video chatting her for her birthday instead of 'enjoying our youth.'"

The corner of Will's mouth ticks. "She even hung up on us, if you can believe it."

I chuckle, but the sound is drowned out by a biker butchering the lyrics of some eighties song. "She figured out how to use the buttons this time?"

Will shakes his head. "It took ten minutes of very patient explaining to help her turn the camera around so that we could see her and not the kitchen table."

"Which, obviously, I left to Will," Bellamy says. "Who also doesn't know he has volunteered to be my designated driver for the evening."

"I assumed that was the case when you shoved the keys

into my hands and flung yourself at the passenger door," Will deadpans.

Bellamy holds up his hands in a shrug and gives us both his best innocent face.

"Did Elena like her card?" I ask, making a mental note to give her a call tomorrow to catch up.

"Loved it, of course," Will says confidently. "Especially because her landscape is way bigger than the one you gave my dad for Father's Day. She thinks it translates to her being your favorite."

"Obviously," I say with a grin.

"We all have our own Cameron originals now," Bellamy says, tapping his exposed tattoo. "Mine's just better than everyone else's."

I smile at my work that's permanently embedded in his skin.

"Cameron," Tori says, stepping toward us a little wobbly before putting her arm around my shoulders. "Are we doing 'Dancing Queen' or what?"

"Absolutely not," I say, shrugging out of her enthusiastic hold. "But I'll be your biggest supporter from afar."

"Cameron," she whines.

But I'm guessing the look on my face confirms I'm not going to budge on this because she, instead, offers a pleading look to Bellamy.

"How about you?" Tori asks him.

"ABBA's not really my thing," he answers.

"I'll give it a go," Will pipes up, surprising every single one of us.

Bellamy balks. "Really?"

"Oh, come on, Mom's made us watch *Mamma Mia!*

enough times that I probably won't even need to look at the lyrics on the screen."

"Perfect," Tori says triumphantly, waving for Will to lead the way to the stage.

Bellamy turns to me with a horrified look on his face. "Should we—"

"Sit on these high stools so we don't miss any of it?" I suggest.

"Yes," he agrees immediately with a nod. "I'll go grab a fresh set of drinks, though."

"Thanks," I say before he heads to the bar.

I keep my gaze fixed toward the side of the stage where Will seems comfortable enough under the slightly dimmed lights of the space, happily chatting with Tori.

Although I'm wildly entertained by the idea of him doing karaoke, I'm more proud to see the confidence within him to do it. It's nice to see that the energetic, bold kid I met before the accident is still inside him, making an occasional appearance when he's up for it.

I smile at the collection of memories in my mind until Will catches my gaze, offering a little wave and grin.

I swear I can feel my *soul* warming at the gesture, and it's something I cling to as Tori captures his attention once again.

It's probably not in my best interest to get caught staring at him a second time, so I grab a napkin from the holder at the end of the table. The pen I dig out of the bottom of my purse isn't my preferred tool for drawing, but it'll do to help pass the time.

I've read a lot of essays and books about art theory and

inspiration enough to know that some people stick to one art form and master it.

But I've always found that if I start with what I know, I can create anything I want.

I draw Will's scar, the same one that's currently slightly covered by his hair, then add some loops and twists and turns.

It's not easy to draw on the flimsy paper napkin, so I turn my pen to the side, adding some depth and shading it out.

"Sorry," Bellamy says, interrupting my creativity by sliding a bottle of root beer in my direction.

I blink as I focus on him. "Sorry for what?"

He eyes the now very detailed piece I've created. "I got caught up with Caitlin for a bit."

"You know her, too?" I ask with a groan. "What about the crew and counselor rivalry? Does no one care about tradition?"

Bellamy laughs. "Well, prepare to feel the very deep betrayal of my actions because she and I made out last summer. She and Brody were on a break, and it was a whole thing."

I consider myself to be a fairly observant person, but both of those pieces of information are new and take me by surprise.

"What?" I nearly shriek. "You didn't tell me that."

"Do you tell me every little thing that happens in your love life?" Bellamy retorts as he twists the cap off his drink.

I glare at him. "Yes. Of course. You know that."

"Well, you're in the minority here," Bellamy says, gesturing to the happy, carefree faces around us.

"Are you saying that in terms of my experience or kissing and telling?" I ask him curiously.

He shakes his head as he traces the label on the bottle. "Well, both, but that's not what I meant."

"I don't get what you're saying," I admit, confused.

"I don't either," he says as his cheeks redden.

Bellamy sways, a bit offbeat to the background music, and I sit back slightly to take in his demeanor.

"Are you drunk?" I ask incredulously. "How long were you talking to Caitlin?"

He laughs for a beat too long. "I don't know. Maybe a little tipsy. She had her own flask and just kept talking and talking and talking about how great Brody is and how she didn't want it to be weird between us. I just kept nodding along and drinking."

"Was it?" I ask.

"Was what what?"

I roll my eyes. "Was it weird? Talking to her?"

"Oh, not really," Bellamy breathes. "And now I'm relaxed and fuzzy, so that's good."

I shake my head, but as the familiar music track picks up, we—along with the rest of the Camp Creek group—turn toward the stage as Will and Tori start belting out the lyrics.

I already know that Will doesn't have a half-bad voice, courtesy of all the times I've heard him sing along with the car radio.

But Tori is absolutely horrific.

She's wildly off-key and stumbles over most of the words, but she doesn't care.

And neither does anyone else, apparently.

Because she appears to be enthralling a group of men standing beside the speaker, and they practically drool as she starts dancing. The sway of her hips and the way she bounces on the balls of her feet is enough to cancel out everything else.

The entire crowd slowly joins in on vocals, adding a range of voices and talent to the song, and even the bartender happily jumps in, lending his voice toward the end.

The Camp Creek crowd rushes toward the stage as the song fades out.

The guy manning the karaoke machine doesn't allow the next people to get on just yet, not wanting to ruin the happy mood of all the people in the bar by changing the style of music.

"I'm going in," Bellamy tells me.

Before I can respond, he jumps to his feet and forces his way into the middle of the crowd where Will and Tori are laughing and dancing.

I smile at his disappearing form before I flip the napkin over, giving myself a blank canvas to start sketching the crowd to stay occupied.

My hand moves on, and I don't capture the faces, just the outline of the mass of people that I refuse to join.

I sip my root beer slowly, letting the bubbles and sweetness coat my tongue as I incorporate some other details of the bar to frame the scene.

My eyes linger over Will, who is doing his favorite robot moves in tune with the beat, which I'm pretty sure I taught him how to do in middle school. He captures the attention of several counselors, three of whom attempt to dance just a *little* more closely to him.

"Why don't you do something about it?" Tori asks, appearing out of nowhere and reaching over to help herself to my drink.

"What?" I reply dumbly.

She levels her gaze at me. "Will."

I continue to project innocence. "What about him?"

"Cameron," she says slowly. "I can tell you like him. But instead of getting out there or doing anything about it, you're sitting here by yourself pining away."

My poker face, as Bellamy has pointed out on multiple occasions, is pretty terrible.

And while I wish I could deny what she's so clearly picked up on, I don't bother lying.

"I tried," I admit with a frown.

Her eyes widen before she takes another pull from the bottle. "For real? What happened? When was this? What'd he say?"

I drop my gaze to the tabletop as I crumple up the napkin. "Last summer. On the last day of camp, it was just him and me in the mess hall. I don't know where Bellamy was at the time, but I just looked at Will and it kind of all spilled out. How long I've felt this way. How I wanted to be more than friends. And how I was hoping he felt the same..."

"And what did he say?" Tori prompts.

I manage a hollow chuckle at the recollection of his panicked expression. "That he just wanted to stay friends. Said it was 'better that way' or something. For a while I wondered if it's because our parents are so close or something like that, but it's taken me even more time to understand that he just doesn't see me that way."

I don't mention how every single time I think about that exchange, I mentally squirm in discomfort and swim in sadness.

Tori tilts her head as she assesses my declaration. "So, what...you've just been staring at him from afar ever since?"

I shake my head. "No, I avoided him for a few weeks after that, and when school started up again, I tried to move on. I even started dating this guy Mike from my calculus class."

"What happened to him?"

"Well, considering I talk about him in the past tense—"

Tori gasps. "He's dead?"

"No," I correct immediately. "We're just not together anymore. Had a pretty good run, though. Did all the dances and first milestones and all that."

She doesn't react other than a slight narrowing of her eyes. "You and Will are inevitable."

I pause, then ultimately sigh. "I hoped we would be."

"I think you two are just beating a dead bush," she says seriously.

At that, I let out a smile. "Do you mean dead bush or a dead horse?"

Tori looks at me like I've grown a second head. "A horse? That's awful. What a foul mental picture."

"Pun intended? Get it? Foal and foul..." I shake it off and tuck my hair behind my ears. "Anyway, the moral of the story is that Will and I are not a thing, and there are no plans to change that. Even if he was interested, if it didn't work out, the damage would be detrimental."

"So dramatic, Cameron," Tori says ominously. "Not something I expected out of you."

"No, you don't understand," I continue. "It makes sense. I mean, our families are really close. Elena, Will and Bellamy's mom, is like another parent to me. So if I did get with Will and we broke up, it would kill my dynamic with her."

Tori lets out a puff of air. "Who says you have to break up?"

"Who says we have to get together?" I argue.

"You're hopeless," she scolds, tossing her blonde hair over her shoulder. "But at least we can go dance."

I shake my head and raise my hands to fend her off. "No way."

"Live a little, Cameron," Tori insists, grabbing my wrist.

I try to twist out of her hold. "Stop."

"No," she says playfully.

"I'm not like you," I snap, sounding a little harsher than I mean to.

That, finally, gets her to release me. "What are you talking about?"

I glance around, grateful that all prying eyes and eavesdroppers are preoccupied before I face her head-on.

"This whole confident, dancing, and being 'out there' in the world thing," I say, softening slightly. "It's not me. I admire that about you, Tori, much more than you know, but it's not who I am."

She leans closer to me, ensuring I'm listening before she speaks again.

"Do you know that you intimidate me a little bit?" Tori asks honestly.

"What?" I balk at that as I take in her posture of confidence, standing tall with her hands on her hips. "No way that's possible."

"It is," she continues. "I mean, damn, Cameron. You're so cool and collected, whereas I'm the equivalent of texting in all caps."

I can't help but laugh hysterically at that. "You're funny."

"I know," she says.

Tori flips her hair over her shoulder and waves her hand like she's showing off her humor.

"But just because we're different doesn't mean we're any worse or better people," she continues. "And just because you're not comfortable jumping up and singing karaoke doesn't mean you also have to be the person who hides away all night long."

I chew on my lip, unsure what to say.

"You can still be brilliant and observant and lovesick while letting yourself enjoy a night out with your room-mate," she says with a note of finality as she holds out her palm to me.

Before my brain can argue, I grasp her hand and let my body follow hers.

And it feels *good*.

The idea that I can just exist and be carefree without the past and the future weighing me down is something I could definitely get addicted to—in measured doses.

Tori and I tune out everyone around us as we have little

dance-offs and sing-alongs and break into laughter over and over again.

I just focus on having fun, which seemed impossible not that long ago.

As I catch Bellamy and Will in my peripheral vision, both of them preoccupied with their own moves and jokes, I'm hit with an immediate wave of nostalgia.

It's an odd emotion, given that I'm so in the moment, but I already know that when I look back on this moment in the fall, I'll miss it.

Because change is coming, and as scary as that is, I think the only thing I can do is focus on upholding the promise we made to one another—to make this the summer that's better than all the best ones combined.

FIVE

Unlike my roommate, I wake up with no hangover.

There's no pounding in my head or swirling nausea, which Tori reports she has, but I do have sore limbs from all the erratic movements I made on the makeshift dance floor.

After I finish getting ready, using up a lot of hot water in the shower, I ease the tightness of my muscles by stretching my arms over my head.

The sounds earn an annoyed groan from my roommate before she rolls over and promptly falls back asleep.

I laugh as she snores loudly and try my best to quietly shut the door behind me, ready to focus on the magic of the first day.

For those of us who aren't nursing headaches, the whirl of excitement in anticipation of everyone's arrival is evident.

I wave at the crew members who are unpacking a fresh shipment of climbing ropes and almost run straight into one of the counselors who is carrying an extra mattress toward their cabin.

When I was a camper, I thought it was interesting how we'd all show up from different towns with a wide variety of background stories but somehow, by the end of the season, end up as great friends.

Some of the same faces would return the next year, but it was guaranteed that there'd be a crop of new folks, too, building on existing dynamics and interactions like a fresh layer of paint.

And today, I get to usher it all in.

I'm stationed at the front gate, which means I'm the first person they'll see after a sickening stream of windy roads through the mountains.

I, thankfully, long ago became accustomed to them, and although it seems kind of silly, it makes me ridiculously happy that they're second nature to me now.

I smile as I adjust the welcome banner—which Rebecca asked for my help in commissioning earlier this week—and wave at a few cars, earning two honks before they enter the grounds.

"Cameron," a booming voice calls from behind me.

"Oh, hey, Brody," I return casually as I face him. "You're on front gate duty with me? I thought Caitlin was my partner today."

He grimaces. "Let's just say she's feeling a little under the weather this morning. Not to mention she's in cabin two…"

"Oh no," I groan. "Nothing like the excited screams of liberated seven-year-olds to soothe a hangover."

"That's why I'm grateful to be in cabin nine this year," Brody says, smiling at a big SUV driving through.

"Older and wiser campers," I say knowingly, smiling as a kid presses their nose against the back window of the big vehicle.

"Sure." Brody adjusts the Camp Creek baseball hat on his head, fiddling with the bill to give him the most coverage from the sun. "But with their own set of challenges."

"Right," I acknowledge. "Like sneaking contraband in."

"I don't have the faintest idea what you're talking about," he says innocently.

But neither of us can withhold our grins for long.

"You know, I once got caught with candy in my trunk when I was a camper," I admit as I wave at another car.

He gasps. "You? No way."

"Uh-huh. I bought a big bag of Skittles at the store before we came up and snuck them in."

"Out of all the candy, *that's* what you chose?" Brody says in disbelief.

"You mock, but it was the best choice," I insist. "Chocolate would have been noticeable by scent and the likely melty mess in those warm cabins, but with Skittles, you can hide them in your pockets and sneak to your mouth at any point in the day."

He smirks at me, then smiles at another approaching minivan. "I can see the strategy."

"Better to keep the sugary stuff on my person. I mean, you know those cabins are an ant infestation waiting to happen."

"Ants?" Brody balks. "No way. There are too many stairs

up to our cabin for that nonsense. Their little legs couldn't handle it. Maybe raccoons."

"Gross," I say with a wince.

"Oh, come on, they're cute and fluffy endearing little shits."

"They're trash pandas, Brody. I suppose if you want to get *rabies* or something, then go for it. Hide your chocolate bars under your mattress and between the slats in your shelves. Maybe behind the shower stall in the cabin."

He chuckles and shakes his head. "You've given this a lot of thought."

"All I'm saying is that candy is a better option than chocolate but maybe not as easy to conceal as a flask of tequila," I joke.

"Fair enough," he admits with a grin.

Our banter continues as we direct a few more cars in, then suddenly, an approaching black sedan pulls off to the side of the road, tires squealing before coming to a stop.

I glance at Brody, who gives me a concerned look before I set off, walking quickly toward the arrivals.

"You looking for Camp Creek?" I call as the mother gets out from behind the wheel.

She lets out something between a groan and a sigh. "Yes, that's where we're headed."

I see the lines of frustration around her eyes and the general exhaustion in her posture.

"Is everything okay?" I ask tentatively.

"It's just...my daughter," she says with a tight smile before lowering her voice. "She's a little nervous."

"Right," I say, tucking my hair behind my ears. "I totally understand."

She opens the back door to reveal a pouting little girl with perfect little blonde ringlets who is definitely young enough that she'll end up in cabin one or two.

"Mom, I told you, I'm not going," she says defiantly, turning her back to her mother.

The woman glances at me in exasperation.

"I've got this," I tell her, tone resolute.

I make my way around the other side of the car and let myself in, sliding in beside the prospective camper and immediately enjoying the benefits of air-conditioning.

Her arms are crossed over her chest, and I can see the long-ago dried tracks from tears on her face.

"Who are you?" the little girl demands.

She has no choice other than to look at me if she wants to keep her back to her mom, and I use it to my advantage.

"I'm Cameron," I say, offering my hand.

I don't actually know if kids that age do handshakes, but I'm willing to try anything to get her to soften and not look so absolutely terrified.

She glances at me skeptically, taking in the Camp Creek shirt I'm wearing. "I'm Eden."

"Nice to meet you, Eden," I say as she squeezes my hand.

She lets go of my grasp after three up and down movements, then goes back to her cross-armed posture.

I let the silence sit for a beat before I attempt to engage her again. "So, what's this I hear about you not wanting to go to camp?"

Eden shakes her head. "I don't want to go, and I'm not going."

"And why not?" I press, catching her mother's frown over her shoulder.

"Because I don't want to."

"Well, it'd be a real shame if you didn't come," I start.

Eden gazes at me skeptically. "Why?"

I let out an exaggerated breath. "I mean, you'd miss out on dessert twice a day, a huge pool, not to mention the overnight camping trip..."

"Don't need them," she huffs stubbornly.

But I can tell by the way her eyes dart as she processes my words that she's warming up to the idea.

I glance around, trying to come up with anything that will help assuage her, and it's then that I notice the bags at her feet. They're overstuffed pouches with crayons, colored pencils, and markers, and it's clear the supplies are well loved and meticulously organized.

I nearly melt at the realization and decide to try to engage her again.

"Well, you see, Eden. I was *really* hoping that someone would be able to help me out in the art cabin this summer, and it's just a shame I haven't found anyone for the job yet."

"Art cabin?" Eden repeats.

"I'm in charge of the program this summer," I explain. "And I have *so* many paints and markers and brushes that I just don't know what to do with."

Eden glances at her mother, then back at me. "Well, maybe I could help you."

I widen my eyes on purpose. "I couldn't ask you to do that. You're not even sure if you want to come yet, and I mean, this would require a fair amount of sitting and drawing and testing out new colors..."

"I'll do it!" Eden says, bouncing in her seat a little.

"I don't know," I say, faking reluctance. "I mean, the person I'm looking for has to be an active participant in *all* camp activities."

"Stop dragging this out," Eden demands with a raised fist. "I said I'm in."

Her mother and I both chuckle, soon joined by the deep rumble of Brody's laughter, signaling his approach.

"Who are you?" Eden asks him skeptically.

"Brody," he returns. "Camp counselor of one of the older boys' cabins."

She glares up at him, not impressed. "Okay."

"You're going to be late if you don't get going," I jump in. "I mean, you want to pick your bunk before too many other kids get here, don't you?"

"Yes," she says, legs swinging. "Mom, can we go now?"

"Of course."

I smile at them both before I climb out. "I'll be seeing you, Eden."

"See you!"

She waves as I shut the door and move back to my post.

"Thank you," her mother mouths, relief evident as she drops back into the driver's seat.

I watch them pull away and shake my head. "I can't believe that worked," I admit to Brody.

"That was surprising," he agrees. "Like some *Karate Kid* Mr. Miyagi or *Star Wars* Jedi mind trickery."

"Or just...art kid relatability?" I suggest.

"Maybe," he allows, stretching his arms up. "Oh, look,

there's Will and Caitlin now."

My heart skips a beat at Will looking adorably sleep-deprived and disheveled.

"Thank goodness," I say, feigning normalcy as they approach.

"Hey, guys!" Caitlin calls, then grimaces at the sound of her own voice. "Am I the only one who feels like living death?"

Brody presses a kiss to her forehead when she reaches us, then hands her his massive water jug. "You can keep this out here."

"Thanks," she says, squeezing his waist before accepting the gift of hydration. "You all good, Cameron?"

"Yeah, I am," I answer. "I had to drive Tori back last night, so I stuck to water and pop."

"I should have done the same," she says as she takes a sip of water.

"Well, I think I'm going to head back," I announce after a beat. "I'm ready to get out of the sun for a little while."

Brody glances at me. "You do look a little pale."

I hold out my arms and twist them. "It's my natural state, achieved from a delicate routine of sitting indoors and avoiding sunshine."

"You artist types sure know how to have a good time," Brody says sarcastically.

Will clears his throat. "Bellamy made *ropa vieja* for lunch today," he says for my benefit.

I feel my eyes widen. "No way. How'd he pull that off?"

Caitlin and Brody exchange a look of confusion before they start chatting in low tones.

"Not sure," he says with a shrug. "He'd probably say

it's the privilege of being the boss or something."

"Definitely," I agree, chuckling. "Our very power-hungry Bellamy."

"I think we better keep an eye on him this summer. Before we know it, Camp Creek will be bankrupt with all of his experimenting and culinary prowess."

"At least we'd be fed very well before he got fired."

Will smiles and checks his watch. "Well, you better go get some before lunch is over."

"Thanks, Will," I say gratefully before I take off.

I'm still clinging to my resolution last night to not allow myself to read into our conversations or feeling any sort of way other than friendship and fun and memory-making.

It's almost too easy to force my attention to simply enjoying the walk.

The main road down the center of camp seems like the most logical way to go, but after lots of time and exploring, I know that this gravel path through the trees will get me there much faster.

My stomach rumbles, encouraging me forward at the thought of the meal ahead.

"What is ropa vay ha?" Brody asks, jogging to catch up with me.

I expected him to stay out with Caitlin for a little while longer, but I don't mind the company.

"It's a Cuban dish," I explain to him. "It's one of their dad's favorite recipes. Meat and vegetables and rice, which sounds boring, but the way it's cooked and the amount of spices and the flavor...it's unbelievable. Trust me."

"Right," he says, nonplussed.

"It actually means 'old clothes,'" I continue as the mess

hall appears between the trees. "It got named that because the meat is served in a way that leaves it kind of long and shredded—"

"Is this you trying to convince me?" Brody asks, one eyebrow arched. "Because it doesn't sound any more appealing."

"More for me then," I say with a shrug.

"You go enjoy that," he says, looking a little peckish. "I should probably go check in with my co-counselor to make sure there aren't any fights over assignments or bunks or shelves."

"Bye," I call after him as I open the screen door.

The mess hall itself is deserted, but the kitchen is bustling with all the volunteers hand chopping vegetables, stirring massive pots, and sautéing something that smells garlicky and delicious.

I inhale the scent of spices and baked bread, a mixture of what was prepared for lunch and what they're working on for dinner.

"I'll be out in a second," Bellamy calls to me from behind the counter. "You hungry?"

"For *ropa vieja*?" I respond eagerly. "Always."

He laughs and refocuses on his task at hand, pulling long strips of aluminum to cover the metal pans of whatever we're having for dinner.

I take a seat on the same bench I always do, grateful to be off my feet for a little while, and appreciate the calm before the storm.

Tonight is the first night everyone eats here in this space together for the official welcome dinner.

We'll all stuff our faces before Rebecca and Matthew

make their welcoming announcements, then we're all sent off for an early lights-out for the campers to recover from travel and prepare for the first full day of activities tomorrow.

After I eat lunch today, I'll head over to the art cabin to ensure everything is just the way I left it, stations already set and prepped for the first batch of campers tomorrow.

"Here you are, my dear," Bellamy says, dropping a plate in front of me.

My mouth waters at the sight. "Thank you so much, Bellamy. I can't believe you managed this today."

He shrugs as he takes the seat across from me. "I figured it'd be good to have one final fantastic meal since we'll move on to the generic, kid-approved foods for the rest of summer."

I laugh, then take my first bite.

It's a little hot, so I have to blow air out of the corner of my mouth to keep from spitting out my food, but I don't care, simply enjoying every single flavor I can pick out.

"Here," he says, offering me a glass of juice to chase it down with.

It helps the heat, but it muddles the flavor, so I'm careful to blow on my next bite before I take it.

"This is incredible," I say with a happy sigh.

Bellamy smiles, but it doesn't fully meet his eyes.

"What's wrong?" I ask, immediately picking up that something's amiss.

"Well, there's actually something I wanted to talk to you about," he hedges.

"Yeah?" I prompt, covering my mouth so I can speak as I chew. "What's up?"

He fidgets slightly, strumming his fingertips on the table. "What's up with Tori?"

I swallow and eye him curiously. "Elaborate, please."

"Like, is she single? Is she interested in me? Or just flirting? What are her plans after camp? What does she like to eat? Do you know her favorite—"

"Bellamy," I interrupt, withholding a laugh at his nervousness. "She's the one who approached you the other day, remember?"

"To get extra food," he argues. "And last night, she seemed to only be interested in dancing with you."

"Because had she not, I would have bolted out of there," I say to him. "You know how much I hate dancing and being around people in general."

He relaxes slightly at that realization. "Oh."

I nod and focus back on my food, forcing myself to slow down and enjoy it instead of shoveling it all in.

"Poor Cameron," Bellamy laments eventually. "The introvert who needs protecting on the big bad dance floor."

I roll my eyes. "Do you want my help with Tori or not?"

He stares me down as a smirk forms on my lips. "Obviously."

"It's going to cost you," I tease him.

"Already got it covered," he says confidently.

Bellamy reaches in his pocket and pulls out one of those little fun size bags of Skittles.

"You didn't," I say excitedly as I reach for it.

"Of course I did," Bellamy retorts. "I know you'd do anything for me and all, but I figured a little sugar on top couldn't hurt."

He's right about that.

SIX

My first few art sessions go off flawlessly.

It's almost too perfect, really.

I start with the older kids, some of who I recognize from prior years, and they want to dive right into brainstorming their big summer projects instead of warming up with the basics.

They have a little more flexibility with what they want to create than the younger kids, who are mostly relegated to using the crafty scissors to create fancy borders around their drawings and finger paintings.

But all the campers, regardless of age, are fascinated by the mural on the ceiling, just like I always have been.

I get an official session with each cabin twice a week, but there are a few chunks of scattered free time where campers can do what they please.

Most of them splash around in the pool or run around on the soccer field, but I know I'll get a handful of campers who will come by the art cabin in those slots and work on their projects or just enjoy the quiet.

Eden approaches me within five minutes of her stepping foot in the art cabin to inform me she'll be here whenever I need her and that she's "ready for duty."

I forgot how many questions inquisitive children can ask and how much attention I'd have to give to ensuring more paint stayed on their projects instead of on their clothing or the floor.

It's a good first day—but a long one.

Finally, during the final time slot of activities before dinner, I get a little break.

It would have been nicer if I could have had this reprieve earlier in the afternoon, but I'll take it when I can.

I watch the cabin three occupants speed off to archery before I take a moment for myself, vowing to figure out how to fit in my own projects as soon as I can.

The space needs to be readied for tomorrow's activities, though, so I busy myself with cleaning up.

I rinse the last of the brushes at the sink, then lay them out on a towel on the counter to dry before glancing out the window, appreciating the slightly pink hues of the sky.

The early signs of the setting sun behind the hills and lake are gorgeous, and it's views like this that make me wish I had gone into photography instead of this type of art.

I doubt I could ever match this stunning shade in paint or pen, especially since it's so fleeting, which is why I've made it a pet project of mine to create the perfect shade of green.

Most people prefer the color blue, choosing their

favorite because it's like the sky and the water, but I think those are a little idyllic. I want to create something that's an homage to the grass and the leaves and the greenery I see every single day from this window, and that's why I've been chasing it for months.

But I suppose I can appreciate the beauty of the lake and how the light reflects off it, mostly because it creates a stunning background for Will's silhouette.

He's enthusiastically introducing himself with lots of arm movements and having the other campers do so, and even from this distance, if I squint I can see his face of concentration as he attempts to memorize all their names in one go.

I think Will is truly in his element in the sun and the water, like it powers him forward in an effortless way.

I can't help but want to get a closer look.

I wipe my hands on a towel and leave my safe haven, letting the door slam shut behind me as I walk carefully down the dirt path toward the beach—if that's even an appropriate term for the tiny area that's a mixture of sand and dirt.

Will grins at me briefly as I approach, but it doesn't break his stride during the big safety speech, a must-hear for all the new campers who would dive headfirst into the lake without a second thought.

I stand off to the side, crossing my arms on my chest to feign the casualness I desperately want to project, and I wait for him to finish.

"And so, to recap, what is the most important part of water sports?" Will asks his slightly restless audience.

"Life jackets," the group of young campers say almost in unison.

Will nods. "And when do we go in the water?"

"Only when we have supervision," they answer.

"And what is better for the soul? A natural, beautiful lake or a chlorinated pool?"

"A natural, beautiful lake."

"Great," Will says, clapping his hands. "Now, my assistant Addison is going to help you all pick out the right size of life jacket, and you're going to practice putting them on, okay? Can everyone say hello to Addison?"

A mixture of "Hello!" and "Hi!" is offered to her.

Addison flashes a big smile at the group as she secures her box braids in a low ponytail. "Let's move," she says, clapping her hands enthusiastically to direct their attention to the shed.

Will steps toward me with a smug look on his face. "Not a bad speech, huh? I'm getting better with each session."

"I take it you're still pissed you didn't get that lifeguard gig last winter?" I tease, bumping his elbow.

"So pissed," he admits with a grin.

I exaggerate a shrug. "Who needs a job at a fancy, indoor swim club, anyway? Who cares if they were paying double the minimum wage? Who even wants free Pilates class coupons?"

Will's shoulders shake as he laughs. "Not me."

"Definitely wasn't hoping to take advantage of the juice bar discount," I say resolutely, shaking my head. "So screw them."

I watch as his laughter tapers off, but his smile stays fixed in place.

"You always say the right thing, you know that?" Will says.

And it's said with such seriousness that I can only assume it's sarcasm.

"I try," I return lightly.

He lets out a long exhale, taking in the view of the sunset before he turns back toward me. "Good first day?"

"Good first day," I confirm, pulling at the hem of my shirt to assess the paint splatters. "Only had to stop one camper from licking one of the scented markers, so I call that a win."

Will snorts. "Life's little victories."

"I'll take them where I can get them."

We stand in silence, side by side, as we take in the sight of the lake and natural beauty around us.

"It feels so good to be back here," he murmurs.

"It does," I say, watching little waves lap at the shore a few feet away. "I can't believe this is our last year, though."

"Or maybe not," Will suggests.

"What?" I balk, slightly alarmed.

"I'm only teasing," he says quickly. "Couldn't you imagine it, though? Spending every summer here, forever. Wouldn't be a bad place to come and recharge."

I gesture toward a group of kids who are becoming progressively rowdier. "If this is your idea of recharging, I think we need to get you checked out at the health clinic or something."

One of the campers makes a big show of putting on a too-small life jacket, then models it for his friends.

"Okay, I can see your point," Will relents with a chuckle. "But, I don't know, I just feel like we're right on the edge of everything changing, and I'm not sure I'm ready for that."

I shove my hands in my pockets. "I get it. It's like I already know that we're living in memories right now. These are the days we'll dream about when we're older."

He nods appreciatively. "That's a great way to put it."

"Is it weird to feel a greater loss at the idea of leaving camp than I did high school?" I ask him.

"If it is, then I'm just as weird as you," Will answers.

I smile. "I'll take it."

He points to the mess of plaster, metal poles, and canvas bunched on the other side of the beach. "Did you see my progress on the sailboat?"

I hesitate because, honestly, it looks infinitely worse than the last time I saw it.

"Wow," I manage out.

"I was going to just repair the hole, but then I noticed that the tiller is a little rusted and the boom doesn't extend fully. I talked to Matthew and Rebecca about it, and they wanted to trash it."

"You talked them out of it, I'm assuming?"

"I did," Will says proudly. "It's going to be my summer project."

"Good for you," I say genuinely.

"Something to leave behind when we're gone, I guess. All the future campers of Camp Creek fighting for a spot on it, setting sail during the perfect summer afternoon."

It's a strange balance, trying to appreciate every moment we have here while feeling like I miss it already.

But I think to truly appreciate what I have in this moment, I have to be aware of what I'm giving up in the future.

Come fall, I'll be in college—hopefully with a kick-ass internship—and far away from the beautiful views and comfort of familiarity offered by Camp Creek.

"You're coming out on the first official sail with me when I'm done, right?" Will asks softly, bringing me back to the present.

I blink in surprise at his request. "Yes, of course."

He's all smiles. "Great."

My phone buzzes in my back pocket, distracting me from just how dazzling I find him.

I pull it out, curious as to who the hell is calling me at all, let alone on the first official day of camp.

"It's Piper," I tell Will with a frown.

"You know if you ignore it, she's just going to keep calling," he warns, watching my finger hover over the decline button.

"You're right," I say, well aware of my sister's habits.

I would much, much rather stay here on a beach—or do anything with Will, really—than endure a conversation with my sister.

But I give in, hoping that if I have a quick conversation now, it will satisfy her for a least a few weeks.

"I'll see you at dinner?" I say to Will as I start to walk up toward the art cabin.

Will nods. "Absolutely. Save me a seat, will you?"

"Of course," I tell him, then swipe to answer the call. "Hi, Piper."

"Cammie! Hi."

I grimace at her use of my nickname, which seems so childish, and her excitement, which is very unnecessary at this moment.

"How's it going?" I ask.

"So great," Piper gushes. "You know how I'm taking that summer class this semester?"

"Macroeconomics, right?"

"Yes! It's so easy. I'm totally going to get an A. But if I had taken it at the main campus this fall, I definitely would have failed. God bless Penn State for accepting these community college transfer credits."

I ease the door closed behind me. "Yeah."

"And did Mom tell you the good news?" she forges on. "About me and TJ?"

To say that I'm not a fan of TJ is the understatement of my life.

But I've kept all comments and thoughts to myself, even the day he "accidentally" sent a risqué picture of himself to me a few months ago.

He claimed it was a mistake.

Piper laughed it off.

But I've been wary of him since that occurrence, paying special attention to how leering he is around me and any other woman with a pulse.

"What about you and TJ?" I ask tentatively.

"We're moving in together!"

Even through the phone, I can practically feel her bouncing up and down with glee.

I squeeze my eyes shut for a moment, physically holding in my immediate response.

"I mean, it's not just us," she amends, oblivious as to

the reason for my silence. "One of his roommates transferred, so there was a spot in his house."

"You're going to live with three other guys?" I clarify.

"Oh, don't make it sound so wild," Piper huffs. "It's going to be great. And so much cheaper than the other places I was looking at."

I absently run my fingertips along the bristles of a few of the half-dried paintbrushes, appreciating the calming softness of the fibers.

"Well, what if you break up?" I pose. "Then you're stuck in a lease together."

"Why would we break up?" Piper asks like it's the furthest possibility that could happen in this world.

"Uh, I don't know," I say quickly. "I'm just looking out."

She laughs into the phone. "Always so worried about me."

It's not exactly *her* I'm worried about in this situation because Piper is strong and independent, but she does have kind of a blind spot when it comes to him.

I think it's because her last few boyfriends have been really standoffish intellectual types, so when TJ, the big hulking linebacker, approached her in the library one afternoon, she was instantly intrigued and smitten.

I can't tell if my parents feel the same way I do about him, but they've always been very supportive and respectful of our decisions—even the little things, like when Piper became a vegetarian and I considered applying to schools abroad.

Still, I wish someone with more life and dating experience than me would weigh in and warn my sister that she's dating a gigantic tool.

"Enough about me," Piper says cheerfully. "How are you? How's your submission for your internship going?"

"It's...going," I say, not very convincingly. "I'm still trying to decide if I want to paint something or draw, but luckily, I have some time before the deadline."

"Well, you'd better get a start on it before you head up to Camp Creek. The last thing you—"

"I'm already here," I interrupt with a frown. "Today's the official first day."

"Oh, wow," Piper says. "Summer is flying by already. It's just like TJ was saying the other day..."

I tune out her boyfriend chatter about his training, their furniture shopping, and some movie he's obsessed with, which continues on uninterrupted for at least ten minutes.

I drop my head back to stare up at the mural, wondering if the person who created this piece had to deal with this kind of banal human interaction while trying to find their creative spark, too.

SEVEN

I immediately forget Piper's encouragement of urgency in regard to my internship submission.

Well, it's not so much that I forget...it's more like I actively purge our conversation from my brain, trying to make room for everything else.

But aside from the fact that I'm not particularly interested in her stories or advice, the first few days of camp fly by so fast that time is a blur.

I imagined that running the arts program would be seamless, easy even, especially after that first day, but it's a lot of work—not just the act of running it but also the prep and thorough cleanup afterward.

I enjoy it, but the days of rinsing and repeating are getting a little monotonous.

And that's not exactly a good sign for the entire summer.

There are so many logistical things I have to consider that I didn't anticipate, such as trying to conserve as much paint as I can without stunting creativity. The goal is to further the longevity of the materials that, in reality, should have all been replaced about two years ago.

"Where do you want these?" Eden asks me, holding up an assortment of round sponges.

"In the basket over there would be great," I answer, directing her with a tilt of my head.

I focus on organizing the table, arranging individual place settings with small easels and wooden palettes.

Eden is a fixture in the art cabin during almost every single free period.

I felt guilt-ridden about it at first, given that she mostly just insists on helping me keep everything organized.

Her time could probably be spent more productively or actively, but she, like me, would much rather be inside with paint on her shirt than running around a soccer field.

And I've come to appreciate the help.

Even outside of my duties in the art cabin, I'm swamped. All the chaperoning and attending of the nightly events put on by Matthew, Rebecca, and a rotating group of the counselors is draining.

This packed schedule doesn't leave me much time to do anything else for myself, let alone think about my own art.

As soon as I lie down on my bed each night, I fall asleep instantly—not until after I make sure to cover my head with my pillow because Tori gets up at an ungodly hour to train and run a few miles before her day even officially starts.

"What are your friends up to?" I ask Eden out of curiosity as I head to the sink to wash my hands.

She shrugs. "Who knows."

I give her a look of disbelief. "I'm sure you do."

"They're learning to canoe," Eden says, trepidation clear.

"And you don't want to do that?" I wager.

Eden nods and busies herself with her task at hand, trying to ignore the question.

It doesn't surprise me at all, given how similar we are.

Not wanting to run around and get dirty is one thing, but on the rare occasion, I have found the water activities kind of tame and somewhat relaxing.

Of course, that might be because I just sit and admire them—and Will—from a distance.

"What about these square sponges?" Eden asks, changing the subject. "Same place?"

"Eden," I say slowly. "Why don't you want to canoe with your friends?"

She keeps her gaze pointed downward. "I just don't want to."

"Are you not getting along?" I press, immediately concerned. "You looked like you were all having fun in here the other day with the collages you're working on. You, Macy, and Kim seem like you're getting along really well."

She finally looks at me, expression a little shy like it was the first day she arrived here. "I'm...scared of the water, and I don't know how to swim."

"Oh," I say in surprise.

"I just never learned, and now it feels like it's too late," she sputters out in a rush. "It's awful. We did the swimming test to be able to go in the deep end of the pool, and I did horrible. All my friends get to practice their dives in the deep end while I have to work on floating near the stairs. It's so embarrassing."

"That's nothing to be ashamed of," I tell her seriously.

She huffs. "Of course you'd say that. You're cool."

I blink, flattered that she would describe me that way, but I keep my attention focused on the issue at hand.

"You know, Eden, it's never too late to start learning something new," I start. "But I have to admit that for most water sports offered here at the lake, you actually don't have to do a lot of swimming."

"What do you mean?" Eden asks skeptically.

"Come on," I say, waving for her to follow me outside the cabin.

She does so without hesitation, which bolsters my pride and deepens my soft spot for her.

I gesture down toward the lake. "What's everyone doing down there?"

"Some people are just standing around on the beach," she answers, squinting ahead. "My friends are really close to crashing their canoes. There's one lady in a kayak nearby…"

"And what are they all wearing?" I prompt.

"Life vests," she answers automatically.

I eye her and nod. "Didn't you listen to that whole lecture on water safety?"

"Yes."

"Then there should be no problem," I say, full of reassurance. "Let's get a closer look."

She follows me, taking three steps for every one of mine.

As we walk toward the beach, we get an even better

view of the water and the trees, and I'm instantly revived by the landscape.

I think it's impossible to get sick of something so beautiful.

"Cameron?" Will calls, jogging over to us as we approach.

I frown at the physical exertion on my behalf.

He eyes Eden and me. "What's going on?"

"Eden here is interested in learning more about water sports that don't require her to swim," I explain.

She's positioned herself a slight step behind me like I'm shielding her from the world.

"Oh, I know Eden," Will says sweetly, offering her a little wave before turning back to me. "I thought you were off tonight?"

"Yes, I am," I tell him.

I originally wasn't supposed to have the night free, but the guy running the archery program asked if I would switch with him, so I agreed to.

I haven't mentioned it to anyone, so I'm curious how he's come across this information.

A bigger part of me is intrigued as to why he is paying such close attention to my schedule.

It's my first official evening without any plans or duties, and it happens to be when no one else is scheduled off with me, so I'm looking forward to a bit of "me time."

It's not like last weekend when Brody and Caitlin had a free night at the same time. They drove an hour away from camp to go out to dinner and do some shopping, taking a list from some of the counselors and crew members with them.

I didn't ask for anything, but Brody handed me a bag of Skittles upon his return, so I couldn't exactly complain.

"Eden!" a few of her friends call out.

She's unable to suppress her small smile, but she doesn't make a move.

"Do you want to sit with me for a while?" Will asks her. "You can keep an eye on your friends if you don't want to join them."

Her eyes widen. "Are you going to work on your sailboat?"

"Oh yeah," he says proudly. "Very exciting stuff. Lots of sanding and reconfiguring and some plaster work."

"Art, really," I tease him.

He offers me a half-smile. "Uh-huh."

"Okay!" She immediately takes off, excitedly perching herself on a log a few feet away from his project.

"Thank you," I say to Will as I back away, relieved of my babysitting duty.

"Anything for you," he tells me, his voice low.

I turn away before I can let myself get excited by those three words, then head back to the art cabin to pick up supplies.

As much as I love the cabin, I'm in the mood for a cozier setting.

I grab what I want, then walk briskly back to Tori's and my domain, happily sprawling out on my bed.

I pop a few of the little candies Brody gifted me into my mouth as I lie back on my pillows, set at just the right height to support my back.

Finally settled, I rub my fingertips over the blank pad of

paper in front of me, like a gentle introduction before I mark it with a piece of charcoal.

Using the material in pencil form is less messy and gives me more control, but I actually prefer the block—it makes shading easier on a large scale. Then again, I don't actually know what I'm creating yet or what kind of shading, if any, I'll need.

Despite spending my days encouraging others' creativity in a beautiful setting, I'm feeling woefully uninspired.

And that's a little devastating.

It's not an absolute necessity to get an internship my freshman year, but it would be huge for my future.

I have no connections to the art world, and I don't really even have an idea of how to turn my passion into a career.

My parents are both dentists, so although they've been tremendously supportive, both financially and emotionally, they're kind of useless about the practical aspect of this sort of thing.

Even my academic advisor barely managed to guide me into the classes she thought might serve as foundation blocks to build a career.

It's shameful that we're expected to know at the age of eighteen how we want to spend the next fifty years. I've never even left the country or met people outside of Pennsylvania before, but somehow I'm supposed to have all the answers for the rest of my life?

While I know that people can always change careers or locations, I still feel that the pressure is on to make a decision now—and invest a terrifying amount of money into my education.

I applied to a few schools, all in-state, but I chose the

university closest to home because it was the one with the most opportunity. It's right in downtown Pittsburgh, which means I can visit museums and galleries whenever I want while still having the benefit of doing laundry at home on the weekends.

Curriculum-wise, there are more classes and mediums and majors to choose from than I expected. I'm not sure if I'll end up going with a hands-on concentration or do something more theoretical like art history.

Which is why landing a semester with a *real* professional who could teach me the ropes and help me figure out exactly how to make a life out of my art would be fantastic.

But first, I have to actually do the work and submit a piece.

There's no prompt or requirement for this, and the ambiguity, I believe, is deliberate, but it's also a little frustrating.

I have no context for what my potential peers are putting together, so I'm just relying on my own instinct as to what feels right.

I put charcoal to paper, and after one simple movement, I'm already not into it. I can't tell if it's because I'm without direction or because I'm not using paint...

But I press on, opening a music app and putting on the latest Dntel album.

Hours pass, and I'm hopeless.

Even the beats and music mastery can't lull me into the right headspace.

I crumple up more wasted paper and toss it across the room. I narrowly miss the bin, but the latest balled-up reject lands on the floor, looking right at home next to Tori's spare cleats and endless piles of clothing, hair ties, and bobby pins.

Before I can stand to retrieve my contribution to the mess—from the side of our space that's immaculate, neat, and organized—Tori calls for me.

She kicks the door open. "Package delivery!"

"Really?" I stand in time for her to hand over a massive box.

"It's heavy," she warns too late.

I stagger under the weight and immediately drop to the floor.

"What's in there?" Tori asks, pulling her hair into a pile on top of her head. "Bricks?"

"I have no idea."

There's no return address, but it doesn't stop me from tearing it open.

I fumble with the hellish amount of packing tape, then pull out a simple card, typed on a piece of computer paper.

Wish we could make it up to Camp Creek to see you. Sending our love and gifts in our place. -Mom & Dad

"I guess this is my parents telling me they're declining my invitation to family weekend," I mutter.

I shuffle through the contents of the box, appreciating the art books but frowning at a few sketchpads that are the wrong size and thickness for the medium I prefer.

Tori sighs and sits on the edge of her bed. "If it makes you feel better, my mom isn't coming up either."

"It doesn't, but thanks," I say with a laugh.

She smiles. "Well, I guess we'll just have to weasel our way into Bellamy's little family get together."

I quirk a brow at her. "Oh yeah? So you admit you're trying to spend more time with him?"

"I admit nothing," she says coyly.

I roll my eyes.

The two of them have been playing this odd cat-and-mouse game since that first day in the mess hall, and while I don't understand the rules or their goals, I'm mildly entertained by it.

Tori once asserted that Will and I were a done deal, but I actually think she was just projecting her dynamic with Bellamy.

"If you need consoling over your parents' rejection, it may interest you to know that I have learned of a stash of ice cream bars in the freezer." Tori wiggles her eyebrows at me. "They're just waiting for two gorgeous young women to take advantage."

"I'm pretty sure those are for the kitchen staff," I tell her.

She stands up and holds her hand out for me. "Maybe they were, but they're ours now."

I sigh as I reach up and accept it, letting her drag me all the way up, then we venture out into the night.

It's just before lights-out, which means the entire camp is quiet and dark, including the mess hall. During the day, it's a hive, bustling with activity at all times, but now, it looks kind of creepy.

"Come on," Tori says, leading me past the counter.

In all my years at Camp Creek, I've never actually crossed this line—being out past curfew and trespassing somewhere I'm clearly not supposed to be—but Tori, so new and fearless, has no trepidation whatsoever about wrenching open the freezer door.

"Ugh, they're ice cream sandwiches, not bars," she groans.

"That's even better," I argue.

"You're crazy."

Still, she hands over a little wrapped rectangle, then takes one for herself before letting the door slam shut.

We have the choice of any table in the room, but out of habit or comfort, I'm not sure which, we make our way over to our usual spot.

The first bite of ice cream sandwich brings back immediate thoughts of my childhood.

There have been far too many times when Will, Bellamy, and I have gorged on the sweet treat, only then to have to try not to get sick while skateboarding around the driveway.

I have so many memories tied up in the Moreno boys that, if I really wanted to, I could connect every meal, movement, and place to some sort of interaction with at least one of them.

And that fact is a major part of why this fall seems so daunting.

Because in a way, I'm not just deciding my own future, I'm building one completely separate from theirs. Will is going to college just down the road from me in the city, but Bellamy's going to Penn State, which is about a four-hour drive from our hometown.

As if I conjured him with my thoughts, Will steps out from behind the counter with a surprised look on his face.

"What are you two doing here?" Will demands.

Bellamy trails behind him, taking in my guilty expression with a smirk. "They're onto our stash."

His twin gasps. "No!"

"Oh, yes." Tori grins, victoriously holding up her half-eaten ice cream sandwich.

"You told me you don't even like these," Bellamy accuses her.

I quirk a brow at her, but she merely shrugs.

"They're not my favorite, but I already polished off those chocolate popsicles you had yesterday," Tori says flippantly.

"I can't believe you all have been holding out on me," I admonish. "I feel *very* betrayed."

Bellamy winces. "Yeah. I guess I have been a little bit."

"Some best friend you are," I tease.

"What about those Skittles you've been hoarding for the past week?" Tori tosses back at me.

My jaw drops open. "You know about those?"

"Yep," she says. "Hard to miss when your mouth is stained like a rainbow every night."

"Don't let her make you feel bad," Will tells me. "The other day Tori ate the last peanut butter brownie. It was an end piece that Bellamy was saving specifically for you."

"How dare you!" Tori scoffs before we all break out into fits of laughter.

It feels good to have this banter and break from my routine, even though it's brief. After a minute, the revelry peters off enough for both Tori and me to finish our treats in a few bites.

"I'll get those for you," Bellamy offers, grabbing our wrappers and tossing them in the right bin.

"How chivalrous," Tori says, fluffing her hair.

"I do what I can," he retorts as he sits back down across from her. "Now, if you both are done, we can—"

"In here!"

Our collective attention snaps to the main entrance, where the too-familiar, booming voice of Matthew rises up from the other side.

On instinct, the four of us dive under the table.

It's a sham of a hiding spot, but it proves somewhat effective when Matthew and Rebecca enter and continue walking past without discovering us.

"I swear I heard voices in here," Matthew insists, shining his flashlight around the room.

Tori shifts slightly, putting all of her weight on my foot, causing me to hiss in pain.

At my sudden intake of breath, Will places his palm over my mouth and pulls me against his chest.

I freeze, afraid that any movement will break the spell of our close proximity, but every single part of me wants to melt into him.

"This is ridiculous, Matthew," Rebecca grumbles. "I'm going to bed."

"So you don't care if we have campers out past curfew?" he snaps back at her.

She sighs. "It's not that I don't care. But as long as there aren't any bears getting into our dry goods, I think we're going to be just fine."

"Bears?" Tori mouths at us with a panicked expression.

Bellamy rolls his eyes and shakes his head. "No," he mouths back.

Matthew laughs sardonically. "And the insurance

liability of a camper who's deathly allergic to nuts getting into, say, peanut butter, and no one finding the child's body until morning? You're 'just fine' with that scenario?"

As Rebecca sputters incredulously, Bellamy bobs his head in impatience, clearly counting the seconds until we're alone again.

But I find I'm quite content at this moment.

The feeling doesn't diminish when Will lowers his hand from my mouth because he leaves one arm wrapped around me.

It's somewhat of an awkward position, but I can feel the rise and fall of his chest.

I can't even imagine how we look from Tori and Bellamy's perspective. It's like he's holding me back from unleashing me on the world, but I couldn't care less.

"I think you're being a little crazy," Rebecca finally tells Matthew. "I'm going to bed now."

He groans. "No, come on..."

A rapid slam of the door and their trailing voices indicate we're in the clear, but we still all give it a beat to make sure they're really gone.

My three friends burst out laughing, but I'm too off-kilter to join in.

"I didn't realize we were competing with wildlife for snacks," Tori says to Bellamy.

He chuckles. "Have you seen your table manners? You're practically half-bear yourself."

"Hey!" Tori says, elbowing him.

She pouts, pretending to be annoyed by his comment, but her eyes twinkle with playful adoration.

Will slowly releases me from his grasp, then clears his

throat. "Let's get out of here before Matthew comes back on a crusade."

"Yeah," Bellamy says. "Agreed."

He and Tori practically roll out from under the table, knocking their limbs together as they move.

Before I scoot out, I glance back at Will, desperately wondering what the hell got into him and what he's thinking.

His expression isn't exactly indecipherable, but I can tell by the way his jaw is clenched and he avoids my gaze that he's not feeling the same things I am.

And I allow myself just a moment of complete selfishness to wish I had as much of an effect on him as he does on me.

EIGHT

It's family weekend, which means although far more people than usual have been entering the gates of Camp Creek, the grounds are nearly empty.

Most campers and their parents are off-site for the day, gorging on delicious fast food, stocking up on whatever they need at the grocery store, or frantically buying more socks and whatever else they need.

There are a few groups scattered around us at tables in the mess hall, laughing and catching up on what's been going on these past few weeks.

With no pen or paper or anything nearby to keep me distracted, I'm stuck watching Tori nervously chew through the manicure I painted for her just this morning.

"You're going to ruin your nails," I scold.

She blinks and abruptly drops her hand, but she doesn't stop fidgeting, wiggling her fingers and nibbling on her bottom lip.

I eye her curiously. "What's going on with you?"

"Do you think that Bellamy's parents are going to like me?" Tori blurts out.

Her concern takes me by surprise.

She's infectiously charismatic, and while I think the Moreno twins and myself are somewhat immune to it, I don't think their parents will be.

"Who doesn't like you?" I ask with a laugh. "Everyone, crew, counselors, campers, loves you the moment they meet you."

"But parents." She lets out a sigh. "I don't know. It just seems so official and daunting."

"Well, what exactly are you being introduced as?" I ask.

"Hell if I know," she says. "Some girl who Bellamy feels up from time to time between meals."

My jaw drops. "You two have been…?"

The shock on my face at least brings a smile to hers.

"Yeah," she says.

"Wow." I pause and take a sip of juice. "That's good."

She quirks a brow. "Is it? You sound uncertain."

"I'm not totally oblivious to you coming back late to our cabin with your shirt on backward," I tell her. "And Eden *has* asked me why Bellamy delivers pitchers of juice to the soccer field but not the art cabin."

"Do you worry about depleting your energy and electrolyte levels while drawing?" Tori asks innocently. "Dehydration really getting to you while you watch a bunch of monsters finger paint?"

I roll my eyes. "Long story short, I'm happy for you two."

"Well, it's not exactly an official thing or anything." She pauses and grins. "But I'm so, so into him."

I return her wide smile easily.

Because the fact that someone feels that way about my best friend makes me absurdly happy.

After all his years of self-doubt and discomfort with his own identity, all I've ever hoped is for Bellamy to find someone who likes him for him.

That elation falters the moment a familiar voice cuts through the light chatter around us.

"Cammie!"

I grimace at that moniker and turn to see my sister beaming at me.

"Piper, what are you doing here?" I say, reluctantly accepting a hug from her.

"We came to see you," she says like it's obvious, flipping a lock of her long brown hair over her shoulder.

"We?" I repeat.

"Hey, Cammie," TJ says as he steps forward.

Before I can react, he wraps his arms around me and lifts me up from the ground.

I think I'm supposed to be delighted by this total invasion of space in the form of a bear hug, but all it does is immediately make me want to take a shower.

"Put me down," I demand as I'm smothered by his limbs and cologne.

His choppy laugh fills my ears as he squeezes me tighter, cutting off my air supply.

When he finally does as I ask, I immediately take a step back, putting clear distance between us.

"I'm Tori, the roommate," she jumps in. "You must be Piper, Cameron's sister?"

"It's so nice to meet you," Piper says genuinely. "This is my boyfriend, TJ."

He doesn't pull Tori in for an embrace, but I see how his eyes linger on her long legs.

She either doesn't see or she ignores his crudeness, and I hope she's not doing the latter for my benefit.

"Join us," she insists, gesturing toward the vacant seats at the table.

Piper sits and pulls TJ down beside her. "Oh my gosh, this place hasn't changed at all."

"You were a camper here?" Tori asks.

My sister smiles as she glances around. "I only lasted one summer," Piper says to Tori. "Roughing it isn't really my thing. But it's pretty charming to see how well Cammie has been doing here."

"She has been doing great," Tori says enthusiastically. "All the kids love her. There's one in particular, Eden, who is, like, sixty pounds of pure spitfire. She's been attached to Cameron during every single free session."

"That sounds like our girl," TJ says, winking at me. "Always taking in strays."

I wrinkle my nose at how creepy and overbearing he is. "That doesn't even make sense," I grumble.

Piper scoffs. "Oh, please. Remember that one time you and Will tried to convince our parents to let you keep that turtle you found by the pond?"

"See?" TJ boasts.

"That was one time," I protest. "And five years ago. You weren't even around then, TJ."

"Whatever," Piper says finally. "Doesn't matter. Tell me

how everything is going. Here and with your art project. Have you created a masterpiece yet?"

I smile flatly. "Good."

"Project?" Tori asks before I can change the subject.

"Yes," Piper answers with glee. "My sister was invited to apply for a *paid* fall internship. Not to mention she's one of only two freshmen given the opportunity to throw a hat in the ring!"

"It's not a big deal," I say to Tori.

"Not a big deal?" Piper repeats incredulously. "It's a huge one, actually."

Tori gives me a questioning glance, no doubt wondering why the hell I haven't told her any of this information.

I avert my gaze immediately, glad that she hasn't unleashed an inquisition in front of my sister and her lame boyfriend.

"Cameron!" a voice calls from the back entrance.

I look up to see the whole Moreno family entering the mess hall, looking as welcoming and at ease as they always do.

"Oh, thank god," I breathe.

I don't even realize I've been holding a stiff and hunched posture, like I'm taking a defensive stance, until I stand up.

My pseudo parents give me a group hug, uncaring that Piper, TJ, and Tori look on awkwardly as they gush over me.

"Cameron, we've missed you so much," Luis tells me once they pull back.

"You look so grown up," Elena says, tucking my hair behind my ears.

I glance down at my appearance—dressed in one of Tori's tank tops and my usual jean shorts—and laugh. "I don't know about that. I think you just haven't seen me in weeks."

"Well, obviously," she says with a smile as she leans closer. "But being in the sun has done wonders for you. Look at all those little freckles."

She pokes at my cheek, and I bat her hands away from my face as lovingly as I can.

Piper clears her throat. "Hi, Mrs. Moreno," she says formally. "It's nice to see you again. And you as well, Mr. Moreno."

"Likewise," Luis says, eyes crinkling in the corners just like Will's do.

"Hello, Piper," Elena returns coolly.

My sister has existed just fine among the Morenos for all these years. It's not like she doesn't get along with them, but she doesn't have the relationship I do with the twins or their parents.

It also probably doesn't help matters that Elena has long been my confidant for all the little petty fights my sister and I have had over the years.

Elena has had my voice in her ear complaining many, many times about my frustrations with Piper and her idiot boyfriend, so the smile doesn't reach the Moreno matriarch's eyes as she takes in the hulking idiot before her.

TJ doesn't even have to open his mouth for any non-smitten person to see there's something off about him. I don't know if it's his smile or over-gelled hair and trendy clothes but sleaziness just radiates.

"And who are you?" Elena asks him in a clipped tone.

I hide my smirk behind Luis's shoulder because his wife knows *exactly* who TJ is.

And judging by her demeanor, she's likely recalling everything I've ever said about him.

"TJ, ma'am," he says politely.

I feel like most mothers would fawn over that politeness and honorific—I know mine did—but Elena does nothing but stare him down.

"I'm Bellamy," my best friend offers. "This is my dad, and this is my brother, Will."

TJ shakes his hand and nods in greeting toward the others.

I watch in horror as he appraises Will up and down, then eyes his scar.

"Oh, yikes, dude," TJ says on a laugh. "You get in a fight or something?"

Will smiles tightly at him. "Something like that."

"I told you," Piper reminds him. "That freak bike accident that happened when we were kids."

TJ's eyes widen as his gaze drops to Will's leg, expecting some mangled limb but getting nothing out of the ordinary.

I grind my molars.

"Right," Elena nods, apparently getting everything she needs from this exchange, and turns to my roommate. "And you are?"

"This is Tori," Bellamy says quickly.

Bellamy waves his hand up and down, gesturing to Tori while giving his mother a pleading look to not embarrass him.

The smile on Elena's face is as wide as I've ever seen it. "Tori."

"It's nice to meet you," my roommate says confidently, grinning at Elena and Luis.

"So, you're the one who has Bellamy all stirred up," Elena drawls.

"Come on, Mom," Bellamy says, cheeks reddening.

"What?" Luis jumps in. "You expect us not to embarrass you when you've talked and texted about her nonstop?"

Elena nods. "I've heard more about her than Cameron this summer."

"What an honor," Tori says with a laugh.

"Hey now," I jump in. "My phone calls don't count for anything?"

Bellamy glares at his parents, then switches to Spanish to chastise his mother.

"Let's have some bug juice," Will suggests, running interference and taking the initiative to rally everyone to sit down.

"Yes," I agree quickly. "Let's."

Our knees knock together as I take the seat across from him, and we frantically pour glasses for all of our guests.

"What is this?" TJ asks, sniffing the cup.

"It's a camp tradition," Piper informs him. "Pretty much just sweetened red dye, I think."

"Right." He drops it on the table. "I have to be careful about my sugar intake, so I think I'll pass."

"Oh," Tori says. "My mom's diabetic, so I understand."

TJ shakes his head. "It's not that. I'm on the football team."

I swear his chest puffs up at the opportunity to brag.

Will's gaze flicks to mine, and in the brief moment our eyes are connected, I swear I have a sense that he's taking in every single thing I'm feeling.

"Oh?" Luis says in interest. "What position?"

Football isn't Luis's thing by any stretch, but it's sweet, I suppose, that he's trying to make conversation.

"Linebacker," TJ replies easily.

I cannot believe my eyes, but he actually flexes his massive bicep.

Luis nods. "That's...great."

"It really is," Piper says, continuing to be overly cheerful. "He's hoping to get drafted when we graduate next year."

"Are you a big football fan?" Tori asks Luis.

"Ah, not really," he admits, offering an apologetic look to TJ.

"He's been trying to get all of us to watch boxing with him for years," I explain to Tori. "Which I definitely like better than the baseball Elena's obsessed with."

"You weren't complaining when I took you to that game last year," Elena says. "In fact, I recall you being *very* enthusiastic about how good our seats were."

"Because it was the fanciest place I'd ever sat in," I remind her. "And the candy was all free and endless."

Most of the table laughs at my admission.

"I love baseball," Tori tells her.

Elena brightens. "Really?"

She nods. "I played softball growing up. Well, I played pretty much every sport, but soccer is what stuck."

"Right," Elena says. "You're playing in college this fall, too?"

"Yes, that's right." Tori sets her hands on the table, finally appearing at ease. "I took this gig here to stay on track with conditioning and bide my time before school starts, but I'm going right from here to official training camp."

TJ snorts and leans his elbows on the table. "Where at? Some little division three school around here?"

Her eyes narrow at his attitude, and she purses her lips before she answers. "I got a full-ride scholarship to Penn State, actually."

Bellamy chokes on his bug juice.

I don't blame him because if I was taking a sip, my reaction might be similar—I knew Tori was good, of course, but I didn't realize she was *that* good.

The look of smugness falls off TJ's face so fast that I wish I had my phone out to record this conversation.

"You okay, Bellamy?" Tori teases as he pounds his chest.

"Fine," he says after a final cough.

"Bellamy is going to the main campus, too," Will supplies. "And that's where Piper and TJ are."

Tori's eyes widen in understanding, then she smirks at Bellamy. "I wonder why this never came up until now."

"That's fantastic that you are going to be in the same place," Elena says, holding her hands to her heart. "You can continue getting to know each other there."

"That would be fun," my roommate agrees.

Elena smiles and shrugs her shoulders. "Maybe even move out of the friendzone?"

"I want to go throw myself in the lake," Bellamy mumbles as he rubs the back of his neck.

Tori howls with laughter. "I don't think that's where we are, technically speaking."

"Definitely not," I agree.

TJ clears his throat because, apparently, he can't help himself but comment on every little thing in this conversation. "So it doesn't bother you that Bellamy is…"

"Cuban?" Tori poses innocently. "No. We're both just who we are. It's not like it bothers him that I'm practically a baby giraffe."

Bellamy grins. "It's a bonus, actually."

"But us short ladies are worth getting a neck cramp for, am I right?" Elena says to me.

"I'll have to survey my next victim and ask," I say lightly.

I risk a glance at Will, trying to see if he has *any* reaction to those words, but his focus, rightfully so, is on TJ.

It's a rarity to see any of the Morenos legitimately angry, and thinking about it now, I don't believe I've seen anything close to that emotion since the three of us shattered one of Elena's prized dish sets.

But looking at Will's murderous expression, how it twists and tightens all of his features, is actually a little frightening.

And oddly exhilarating.

"No," TJ presses. "I mean—"

"Well, I could do without his and Will's secret Spanish conversations," Tori inserts breezily. "But it's fine."

"I mean that he's trans," TJ says a little venomously. "You're fine with it?"

Tori turns to face him head-on, squaring her shoulders. "I don't care in the least," she says slowly and deliberately.

I know Bellamy doesn't mind curiosity or even clarifying questions, using it as a moment to educate and explain gently, but I know enough about TJ to know that he's not asking to bring about inclusivity or better understanding.

He's just being an asshole.

TJ's eyes roam briefly, noting everyone frozen around us, but he doesn't let it go. "So, just to be clear, you don't care that he was once…not a he?"

But before any of us can jump in, Tori comes up with an expert-level response. "I just find it fascinating that you're so interested in another person's genitalia. Do you regularly spend your time thinking about other men's penises?"

TJ sputters. "No way. I'm not some—"

Before he can spew some slurs or bullshit, I cut him off. "That's enough," I say venomously, slapping both hands on the table.

Our entire party is stunned by my outburst—no one more so than myself, honestly—but I don't lose my resolve.

"You don't get to come here, uninvited I might add, and dump all of your prejudice and narrow-minded bullshit on us," I continue, rage dripping from my tone. "You should go."

TJ lets out a nervous laugh. "I was just asking questions."

I shake my head. "If that was the case, we wouldn't have any problems," I say as evenly as I can muster.

"Oh, come on, you're being ridiculous," he says, gazing

around the table like he's waiting for someone to speak up on his behalf.

I don't even bother waiting for him to look at me before I speak again because now that I've started, I can't stop the truth from tumbling out. "Aside from that, you've insulted almost everyone at this table. Commenting on Will's scar… leering at Tori…and I don't believe for one second that you sending me *that* traumatizing picture was accidental."

Elena covers her laugh with a cough.

"I both hate and love to be the one to tell you this, but you're actually the absolute worst person I've ever encountered." I pause for emphasis. "Please leave. I don't ever want to see your face again."

"Cameron," Piper, finally finding her voice again, admonishes in disbelief.

I turn to her and frown. "And you're an idiot for not seeing it yourself, Piper. I can't believe I have blood relation to someone who would find someone like him appealing in any way."

Piper opens and closes her mouth a few times.

I stand up so violently that my hips hit the table, splashing some of my drink on the tabletop. "I'll see you both out."

TJ glances at Piper, who looks absolutely shell-shocked.

"Now," I repeat.

They both wordlessly follow me toward the exit without looking back.

Just before I step out the door, I hear Bellamy clear his throat. "More bug juice, anyone?"

NINE

"I knew I'd find you here."

Under normal circumstances, my heart would soar that Will has hunted me down.

But as he hops up on the counter just to the left of my easel and sopping wet canvas, I let out a noncommittal huff.

When I stormed away from Piper's car, my feet moved on autopilot, bringing me to this very spot. I spent at least an hour lying on the floor and staring up at the mural before I felt the urge to put a brush in my own hand.

I don't think it's the norm for artists to love two mediums equally, but I feel just as comfortable with paint as I do with charcoal.

In fact, it's somewhat of a perk that I'm able to switch between the two, choosing the right material to convey whatever is in my brain.

Today, it's a swirl of black and white paint.

The jagged line representing the one on Will's face is

already covered with layers, mixed to a sort of muted gray before I began adding other definition to it.

Taking inspiration from above, literally, I've created an angel, but I've added my own twist.

The heavenly being is supposed to be all white with a long, flowy dress, equally stunning hair, and big, beautiful wings, but my depiction is not as glorious.

It's somewhat dark, violent even, with slashes of paint.

I don't even know what I'm trying to say here or what this means, but in place of feathered appendages, I've created two waves to jut out from the back of the angel and lap the edges of the canvas. My take on "wings" are what I've blended my trademark jagged line into.

"This is beautiful," Will murmurs, eyeing the piece carefully.

I finally set down my brush and turn to look at him, frowning as I notice he's hiding the left side of his face, even though it's just us.

It makes me angry all over again.

TJ is such a prick on so many levels. I've tolerated his presence for Piper's benefit, even though he's always made me uncomfortable. But now that he's outwardly being awful to the two people I love most in this world...I'm not having it.

The damage done by his words makes me even more devastated for Will, who wants to be so much more than "the guy with the scar."

He doesn't know he already is to me.

"Thank you," I return quietly.

Will nods and presses his hands against the edge of the counter surface, leaning forward to get a better look at what I've created. "Is this what you're going to submit for your internship?"

"I haven't decided yet."

"But the deadline is coming up soon, right? Before camp ends?"

I suck my bottom lip between my teeth, realizing that is way sooner than I want it to be.

The summer's already half-over.

Perhaps noting my shift in mood, Will points up at one of the walls to where I've hung some of my other doodles and paintings from this summer.

"What's that one?"

I follow his gaze, taking in a canvas with about fifty dots of different greens on it. "Eden and I are on a quest."

"A quest?" he asks, crossing his arms over his chest. "And you haven't asked me to participate?"

The corner of my mouth ticks. "I'm trying to create the best shade of green."

"Oh. Still? Like you were a few months ago?" He pauses and squints. "Why?"

I shrug. "It's just a little project I've been working on for a while, and she offered to help."

He gestures to a few half-finished portraits of Bellamy and depictions of what's just outside the art cabin window. "Well, I like the physical record of the attempt, at least. It looks abstract and cool. And I like those other pieces as well."

"I do, too," I admit quietly.

"But you don't want to send any of them in as your submission?" Will asks.

I take a beat to respond. "They just feel too personal."

He gives me a questioning look. "Too personal?"

"I always pour so much of myself into my art, and I've never had an issue with presenting in the past. But for someone else to hold it in their hands and judge it like they're measuring to see if I'm worth something…I don't know." I frown just thinking about it. "Maybe I'm just not cut out to *really* let people see my work."

"What are you talking about?" Will says, confusion evident. "You let me see your stuff all the time."

"But you're not 'people.'" I laugh hollowly. "You're *you*."

That sentence hangs in the air between us.

He clears his throat and pointedly shifts his gaze from my face, looking out the window at the water down below.

"Well, at least you have a good view to inspire you. You can see all the repairs I'm doing on—"

Will stops abruptly, and his eyes brighten as he turns back to me.

"What?" I ask nervously.

"Maybe you just need a change of canvas," he suggests in a rush.

"What are you talking about?"

"My boat could use a new coat of paint."

I withhold an eyeroll. "Are you just trying to get some free labor on your summer project?"

"No," he says forcefully. "Look, all the other people you're up against are probably going to present the same thing you're working on. Something on a boring old canvas. Uh, no offense."

I snort. "None taken."

"But if you reframe your presentation," Will says excitedly. "You could do the bottom of the boat, the sides, hell, whatever part you want."

I turn toward the window, wanting to see what he sees.

"Come on," he insists, reaching for my hand.

I don't get the chance to envision it because I'm helpless to do anything but watch as he threads our fingers together—something I don't think has happened since we were old enough to realize the romantic implications of the gesture.

"Just take a look," he implores.

With our hands intertwined, I don't think there's anything I wouldn't do for him.

I wish this was more than a friendly, comforting gesture, but after all the years of letting my heart sing for our little moments together, reality is finally hitting me.

It's silly that I ever misconstrued his friendship as being something more.

Instead, I'm choosing to be glad that we're strong enough to have moved past my attempt to make us take the next step last summer.

I also ignore the gut reaction to think he's finally ready for more when he squeezes our palms together, reminding me just how perfectly our hands fit together.

But it really feels like they were made to do this and nothing else.

As we come to a stop on the beach, I release myself from his grasp, cross my arms over my chest, and focus my attention on the absolute mess in front of me.

"Will, this is a disaster," I say, turning back to take in his frown.

"It's not that bad," he says defensively.

I step around the wreckage, wondering if he's really trying to fix it. "How am I supposed to work on this when it's half taken apart?"

"Well, now that I have the extra incentive of getting you that internship, I'll pick up the speed on repairs."

I narrow my eyes at him.

"Cameron, really *look* at it," Will says seriously. "If anyone can bring beauty to this shipwreck, it's you."

I crouch down and drag my fingers along the smooth outer edge of the boat.

It'll be difficult to do anything without a coat of primer, but I do love this slight curve. The stroke of the brush would follow it quite nicely.

I could possibly create a whole scene or just add some colors—maybe swirls of blue to blend in with the lake.

The rest of the vessel is pretty standard. The deck is lined with that material that feels like sandpaper, so passengers don't slip, and I think I could add some really cool flecks on top of it, give it some depth.

I fixate on other little details and cracks that need repairing, wondering how I can incorporate them into the design.

Then I sigh and step back.

"I can see it," I admit.

"I knew it," Will says without an ounce of arrogance.

I stretch upward, undoing the damage and tightness from my hunched position. "Thank you."

He shakes his head. "I didn't do anything. You're the visionary."

The little compliments and remarks that show he's

paying attention to me are nice, but it's his unflappable belief in me that makes my heart pound for him.

"Thanks for helping me get out of my head," I say with a small smile.

"Someone had to get you away from the paint fumes for a little while," Will teases. "Fresh air and all that."

I laugh and let the silence settle over us for a bit, enjoying the view.

The lake is gorgeous this time of day, reflecting the sun as it starts to set.

"How is Bellamy?" I ask eventually, unable to escape the lingering emotions from earlier. "Did I ruin family time for both of you?"

"Ruin it? You made it better." Will grins at me. "I've never seen you so livid. Not even when those asshole sophomores were calling Bellamy by his dead name last spring."

"Ignorance is not something I tolerate anytime, but somehow, today just seemed worse. Coming to our safe haven with that bigotry…" I trail off and shake my head.

"He's fine," Will reassures me. "He and Tori are even going out for ice cream instead of sneaking it from the freezer, so that's a victory for today."

"Like a real date?" I ask curiously.

He nods. "A real date."

"Really?"

"Really."

"Huh," I breathe. "Who would have thought? Well, aside from you and me."

"My parents," Will continues, ticking the names off his fingers. "The campers. Everyone in the kitchen. Pretty much anyone who has been within ten feet of them this summer."

I laugh, finally feeling like some of the weight I've let drag me down has let up. "Well, good for them."

"And for us."

I give him a pointed look of confusion. "What do you mean?"

He glances upward. "More sunset for you and me."

TEN

It's pouring.

Actually, that word is an inadequate description because it truly feels like the sky is punishing us all—for what, I'm not sure.

It's the kind of rain that renders an umbrella useless within seconds of trying to face off against the gusts of wind, and the downpour over these last few days makes it feel like we're underwater.

Tori and I only leave the safety of our little space to run to the mess hall, load up with snacks, and sprint back. She, of course, does the actual running while I just succumb to looking like a drowned rat.

One would think that all this time holed up would make me exceedingly productive, but I spend most of the time watching makeup tutorials on YouTube while Tori does rounds of pushups and lunges in our tiny space.

Being cramped up does spur her into a sudden burst of cleanliness, though, so I count that as a win.

On the third day of being stuck inside, Rebecca arrives at our door, announcing that all staff is expected in the mess hall. She's waterproofed from head to toe, dressed as a full-time fisherman who goes scuba diving on the weekends, whereas Tori and I share a garbage bag for cover while we walk.

"God," Tori groans, trying to squeeze the water from her long hair. "We're turning into fish at this point."

I shake my arms, sending little drops of water all over our favorite table. "Might as well be."

"Well, at least everyone looks as miserable as we do," Tori says as we sit down.

"The rain has somewhat subsided," I offer, trying to stay optimistic. "Now, instead of pure violence, it's—"

"A fistfight we're all losing?" Will suggests as he slides in beside me.

I chuckle at that way of putting it. "Yes."

"Well, this should make things a little better," Bellamy says, approaching with a gigantic tray in his hands.

I inhale the buttery scent of baked goods and eye the beautiful blueberry muffins before me.

"Yes, yes it does," Tori confirms, reaching for one immediately.

"You're an angel," I tell Bellamy before I take my first bite.

Tori glances between the Moreno brothers. "Why do you guys look so smug and dry?"

"I don't know what you're referring to," Bellamy says innocently.

He takes the seat beside her—a rare move, considering

he's usually behind the counter and ordering people around in the kitchen.

"Not buying it," she says after swallowing a sizable bite. "Although, these are a delicious distraction."

"The same could be said about me," Bellamy retorts.

Tori lets out a somewhat uncharacteristic giggle, and I glance at Will, who smiles and shakes his head.

"Attention, attention," Rebecca calls out from where she stands between all the occupied tables.

I glance around quickly, noting that the entire crew is in attendance.

I see only half the counselors, which makes sense, since some of them have to stay behind to watch the campers, and I *almost* pity them. If being stuck in a room with Tori for days induces a sense of mild cabin fever, I can't even imagine how they're faring.

"At least Matthew isn't here," Tori says quietly. "That guy is so obnoxious."

"He would probably melt in the rain," Will mumbles.

I turn to him. "Did you just make a *Wizard of Oz* reference?"

"Maybe," he says, the corners of his mouth twitching.

"That's two musicals in one summer," I remind him. "Do you have some Broadway infatuation I don't know about?"

"You don't know everything about me," Will says lightly, tone teasing.

"Are you sure about that?" I challenge.

"Uh-huh," he breathes.

I quirk a brow.

He pointedly keeps his gaze forward in an attempt not

to lose the argument. "You're keeping me from hearing these very important announcements."

I roll my eyes and focus on Rebecca's words once more.

"Frankly, we're running out of ideas," she says seriously. "As you can see, we've stopped the flow of water from coming directly into the mess hall. But Matthew is currently trying to do damage control in the rec area. Two nights ago, the wind blew over the projector and tangled our climbing ropes. And we can't even locate the volleyball net."

I can't help but inwardly laugh at the visual of Matthew frantically chasing down various Camp Creek items.

"So," Rebecca says with a sigh, "does anyone have a thought about how we can entertain our visitors until the rain lets up?"

"How about board games here in the mess hall?" Caitlin suggests. "All my campers have been playing cards and building forts in the cabins, and they could use a change of scenery."

"And make the cleanup crew deal with all the mud that a bunch of ten-year-olds will inevitably trek in here?" Bellamy retorts. "Not happening."

Caitlin gives him an exasperated look. "Oh, come on. The space is huge, and us counselors could use a break."

"We can barely keep this space clean during regular camp life." He shudders at the thought. "Hard pass."

I love that Bellamy, who is even more of a neat freak than I am, is completely unaware that Tori is perhaps the messiest person I've ever encountered.

"Surely there's a happy medium here," Rebecca coaxes, glancing around to the rest of us.

Tori wipes her mouth with the back of her hand to ensure there are no crumbs before she speaks. "Wait," she says loudly. "I think I have an idea."

Rebecca's eyes brighten. "Yes?"

"Some of the most fun I've ever had was when I was on a traveling team in junior high. We had a big tournament one weekend, and it *poured* for days before. Since it wasn't storming on the actual day of the games, we had to play. The field was a total mud pit, but it was, like, unbelievably fun."

"Sounds great," Bellamy chimes in. "As long as it's far, far away from here."

"But not everyone likes soccer," Caitlin argues.

"I'm down," Brody shrugs, earning a glare from his girlfriend. "Oh, come on. I'll do anything to not be cooped up any longer."

"We can do a bunch of activities," Tori continues. "We can incorporate all the regular things offered here at Camp Creek. Right, Cameron?"

"Uh, yeah. Definitely." I pause as I wrack my brain. "Mud painting is actually one of the earliest practiced art forms. We could make it work."

"See?" Tori says. "And we can do just about everything else. Soccer, basketball, hockey, volleyball. If the net is recovered, that is."

"Maybe not archery, though," Will adds lightly. "But we could definitely do something by the beach and at the very edge of the water."

Tori laughs. "So what do you think, Rebecca? Does this sound like a plan?"

Rebecca smiles, looking both thrilled and relieved. "I think we have just created our first annual Mud Games."

———

The Mud Games are, without a fraction of a doubt, a hit.

It's not that I didn't believe in Tori's vision, but I was skeptical about how entertained several hundred kids could be by the dirt and rain.

In short, I severely underestimated the entire endeavor.

The elation of breaking through cabin fever was one thing, but the blanket permission to jump in puddles and get messy? I don't think I've ever seen so many smiles at once.

Most of the children are barefoot and wearing bathing suits—and several of them also put on swim caps to protect their hair—but a few are weighed down by now-water-logged clothing and sneakers.

"Come on, Eden," one of the other campers calls.

Eden glances up at me through the mud caked over nearly her entire person, wearing a look of hesitation.

"Go ahead," I encourage her.

"But what about the flowers?" Eden asks tentatively.

We've spent the better part of an hour trying to success-fully stick little daisies on the side of the art cabin with mud. We've had only moderate success with the endeavor because while the rain has lessened, it's still moving in the direction of the biggest blank wall, washing away most of our efforts.

"It'll be fine," I promise. "We can always just try this with regular paint some other time."

I'm not sure if Matthew would be okay with us giving the exterior a new look, but we can always put up temporary slats of wood or something.

"But it'll look uneven if we don't finish now," Eden says, panicking. "And what happens if it's all messy when the rain stops? How are we going to clean it? And I haven't checked on the painting I made. Are you *sure* everything is dry inside the cabin? And we still haven't made the perfect shade of green!"

"Eden," I say slowly, channeling the same energy Tori had when she convinced me to join her on the dance floor weeks ago. "You don't have to do everything now."

She frowns at that. "But— "

"You can just enjoy this."

And it's advice I've been trying to do a better job of following myself.

She gives me and the makeshift tunic I'm wearing, made from a garbage bag, another look of uncertainty.

"Go on," I urge.

"Fine," Eden huffs finally before walking away.

I smile at her retreating form and give up on the project of "gluing" daisies to the cabin's exterior walls.

The rain has cleared up enough that I can see how rough the water looks down below, and it's what holds my attention now.

Eventually, the few remaining mud-flinging stragglers hanging around me get lured away by the excitement of running and splashing around in the surrounding mud puddles.

And honestly, I'm not offended at all.

It gives me a chance to wander around in the rain. I

wish it were safe to wear my headphones and listen to music that matches the overcast mood.

Instead, I head over to the basketball court, one of the few outdoor structures with a roof.

There are a dozen campers around, totally soaked and catching their breath.

I wave at a few familiar faces, then stand at the edge of the blacktop court, getting a nice view of Tori and the handful of people attempting to play soccer.

With the humidity, it feels like we're living and breathing in a sauna. The rain is warm, but even so, it is slightly annoying to feel drenched to the bone.

While most of the crew looks to be in the same shape as me, the campers are obviously unfazed, able to give hours and hours of energy to getting dirty without consequence.

"Here," Bellamy says, stepping up beside me.

He shoves something discreetly in my hand, and I lift his offering and gasp.

"Bellamy," I practically groan at the sight of a small packet of Skittles. "Where did you get these?"

"I had to go on a supply run this morning, so I grabbed those for you," he explains. "The rest are hidden in the mess hall."

"You're my savior," I tell him as I pick out a few red ones to pop in my mouth.

"Don't let everyone else see," Bellamy warns playfully. "They'll all be coming after me, and I can barely keep up with your need for sugar."

I laugh before I focus on chewing through the remaining little candies in the pouch.

"I feel so much better already," I tell him. "Thank you."

"Good," he says, wrinkling his nose at the sight of all the mud flying around. "I can't believe I'm dating someone who actually thrives in this type of messy nonsense."

"Dating?" I echo. "Is that what you're finally calling it?"

"Tori said it first, not me," Bellamy tells me like he's defending the use of it. "That whole family weekend 'friendzone' conversation kind of changed things with us."

"It was all Elena?" I postulate, not buying it. "Not the fact that you both discovered you're going to the same college and the dynamic shifted from an ambiguous summer fling to something with actual potential?"

He looks at me with wide eyes, then his features soften. "Something like that."

I nod as I shove the wrapper in my pocket, erasing all traces of evidence of my sugary pick-me-up.

"It's just a little daunting, you know?" Bellamy says softly. "I've never been in a real relationship before, and I think that's where we're headed."

I slip my arm around his waist, giving him a side hug. "Vulnerability is scary as hell."

"So are you," Bellamy jokes as he puts his arm over my shoulders.

"What do you mean?" I ask, genuinely confused by his statement.

"You yelling at TJ like that. It's like you turned into some sort of feral creature." He pauses to let out a chuckle, which I join in on. "I'm flattered that side of you came out on my behalf."

"Yeah, well, our days are numbered, Bellamy," I tell him, only half-joking. "I guess I need to get all my protective best friend instincts out of my system before we go off to college."

"Don't remind me," he says with a sigh.

"We can't avoid it forever," I tell him.

"I know. It's just...why has no one invented teleporting yet?"

"It would be very convenient if one zap could transport me across the state," I agree with him.

"OH HELL NO!" Tori yells, catching our attention and effectively ending our little moment.

A few of the little kids giggle at her cursing, and she instantly realizes her mistake as she tries to remove the glob of mud from her hair.

"Heck!" Tori says quickly. "I said heck."

"No you didn't," one of the campers says before running away.

She and the others have, apparently, given up on a formal soccer game in favor of merely chasing one another around.

Will and the rest of his staff stand near the goal with a group of kids, and after a beat, they all take off running.

And that's when everything dissolves into pure madness.

A full-on mud fight breaks out, with Tori leading one side of the charge and Will the other, using the line marking the two sides of the field as their divider.

The younger kids scream in delight as they run around and slide in puddles, but the older campers are more focused, taking the dodgeball-style fight more seriously.

"Come on, we're going in," Brody announces, voice

booming across the sheltered basketball court as he breezes by us.

"Brody," Caitlin whines as she tugs on his hand, trying to stop him in his tracks. "I'm exhausted."

"All of you," he announces, making eye contact with Bellamy and me. "Stop standing around like boring sad people, and let's join in."

"I actually resent that," Bellamy murmurs.

Brody's words of encouragement work surprisingly well on the remaining crew around us, and they follow him without question.

I'm not convinced that I want to join until I catch a glimpse of Will—his entire face is covered in mud.

All I can see are his eyes and white smile, and I realize I want to feel whatever he is feeling at this moment—not just witness it.

"Come on," I say to Bellamy, elbowing him.

"Absolutely not," he protests firmly.

"Bellamy." I make my voice as serious as I can. "Take a look at Tori right now."

His mouth flattens in annoyance, but he does as I ask.

"See how much fun she's having?"

"Yes."

"I know she looks like that pretty much all the time, especially when she's playing a match, but at this second, you can be a part of it," I continue. "Creating a memory *with* her that's lighthearted and a little messy. Let's go participate instead of just standing on the sidelines."

Bellamy runs a hand over his hair. "Fine."

"Really?" I blink, surprised.

"Yeah. I think you need this, but you're too good of a

friend to leave me behind." He sighs and holds out his hand. "If my binder gets ruined, though, you have to buy me a new one."

"Deal." I accept his grasp, squeezing once. "Love you, Bells."

He smiles. "Love you, too, *Cammie*."

I glare at him before we take off.

Together, we run out into the rain and mess, splashing through the once-pristine grass field.

Our shoes sink with each step. My thighs burn at the effort of trying to stop myself from getting stuck, but eventually, we reach the throng of people.

Tori sprints over and slides like I've seen ice skaters do on television, spraying Bellamy and me with water and dirt, covering our legs in muck.

"Hey!" Bellamy says, recoiling slightly.

She laughs and scoops up some mud with her hands, then tosses it, hitting him square in the chest.

"Oh, you're on," Bellamy growls, then chases after her.

I shake my head at their antics, but I, obviously, love it.

I want the best for both of them, and seeing how happy they make each other, I send all the good vibes in the world that they work everything out—either as friends or something more.

"Cameron," Will calls as he jogs toward me.

He looks as free and light as I've ever seen him, despite the weight of the mud that's covering almost all of him.

"Hey," I say when he's within close proximity.

He tries to mimic Tori's antics of skidding to a stop before me, but he slips. As he wobbles, his hands hit my waist, pulling me into him and completely off-balance.

It's like one of those funny videos where a person tries everything to stop the fall as it happens, and it's futile.

We tumble down, and it's a soft landing for me, sort of, because he hits the ground and I land on top of him.

I get a moment to appreciate our proximity with my cheek against his chest before I let out a groan at the feeling of another human body on top of mine.

Will and I very quickly find ourselves at the bottom of a dogpile.

I squeal as little hands and arms wiggle around me and the pressure of people increases. I definitely hear Brody and Tori yell before the weight increases, and I feel the bouncing of laughter Will lets out.

"Okay," Bellamy says loudly. "That's enough. We don't want to smother anyone to death in the mud."

There are a few reluctant groans, but as Will and I extricate ourselves, we're all immediately caught up in the battle once again, ensuring that no one is spared from the cover of mud.

This goes on for several minutes until it appears that the campers are—finally—losing steam.

I've never been more grateful for exhaustion to set in to other people.

There are still a few troublemakers causing chaos, but the counselors do their best to corral the campers toward the cabins. Smiles are wide as they walk, looking to shower and get some rest before dinner in the mess hall.

Brody, Caitlin, and the other staff members head back to their own designated area, but the four of us—Bellamy, Tori, Will, and me—stay back on the field.

"Well, it's just us now." Tori rubs her hands together as her lips curl into a sinister smile. "Two-on-two mud fight?"

"No," Bellamy says, making the decision for all of us.

I glance around at the destroyed field as the rain continues to peter off, taking in the space until my gaze wanders toward the lake.

I let out a happy sigh as inspiration strikes.

"I think I have a better idea," I admit, pointing toward the hill between the art cabin and the water. "I bet that area could serve as a makeshift slide. We've all got our garbage bags on, and it'll probably be slick enough to work."

Without a word of agreement, Tori takes off in a burst.

The three of us follow her at a much slower pace, but when we finally catch up to her, there's no hesitation.

We all drop and go for it.

As we slide down, all four of us instinctively stay to the left, aiming toward the drop-off that leads directly into the lake instead of the beach. We all let out yelps and laughs as we move.

It's a rush, but it's not exactly smooth sailing.

I feel every single bump of the uneven hill as I go, grateful that my momentum doesn't stop as I ungracefully manage to roll forward. I fall right off the edge of the bank and into the lake with a splash.

The water that welcomes me is cool and somewhat refreshing, even though at this point, I'm not sure I ever want to be wet again.

Bellamy and Tori jump up and chase each other, moving a little deeper into the water.

I choose to sink to my knees into the shallow part, then focus on scrubbing the caked-on dirt from my skin.

Will, the last one to make it down the hill, stands and winces as he moves. His leg appears to be a little stiff after all the activity today.

I frown as he sits down beside me, letting the water lap up to his chest.

"You okay?" I ask.

He ignores my pointed look of concern and nods. "Yeah."

His tone is a little clipped, and I can tell he doesn't want to talk about it.

In the past, I'd press him for details or encourage him to just be honest, but in the spirit of trying to just enjoy the moment, I decide it's better to just carry on and distract him from the obvious pain he feels but won't fess up to.

I tilt my head toward my best friend and my roommate. "Shouldn't the head of aquatics be lecturing them about life vests?" I tease Will.

"I think they can take care of themselves," he says quietly.

Will's definitely right about that, but I don't get the chance to tell him so because he sinks fully in the water. He stretches out his limbs and lets out a few air bubbles in an effort to completely submerge himself.

I check over my own clothes and skin, glad to see that it's mostly clean at this point.

When Will resurfaces, his face is half-clean, but there's a gigantic smudge of wet dirt down his cheek.

"Here," I offer, reaching out without a moment's thought.

The second my thumb hits his skin, he jerks backward and bats my hand away.

"It's fine, Cameron," he says sharply.

He stands a little unsteadily, then heads toward his brother, movements quickening when he's deep enough to use his arms to propel him forward.

I'm momentarily stunned by the abruptness.

It takes me a second to realize that, in all the years we've known each other, that is the first time I've ever actually touched his scar.

To him, I've certainly stepped over a terrifying and vulnerable boundary.

But, in the moment, I didn't even see it—the line I crossed or the one on his face.

ELEVEN

It's been a few days since the Mud Games, and with the exception of the very torn-up soccer field, it's as if it never happened.

The grounds have fully dried out. The destruction has been mostly repaired. The campers are back to their normal schedule of activities.

And I'm *very* aware of how fast the time is passing.

While I'm happy to spend hours inhaling paint fumes and cleaning dozens of brushes, I glance out the window at Will and the slightly repaired sailboat—and start to seriously consider his offer of using it as a canvas.

I tell myself it's definitely not just an attempt to spend more time with him—even though things are totally back to normal after the instinctual scar touching—but it probably is.

But I guess I'm just glad I didn't start before the torrential downpour because it would have probably washed away all my work.

I sketch out my idea during the free period, the time when everyone mills about camp and does their favorite activities.

There are a handful of kids around me, all lost in their own projects, and most of them bop along to the song coming through the speakers of the old radio I only recently found the cord for.

But beside me, Eden continues our quest for the perfect green.

"What if we add more blue?" she asks, staring at our palette.

"It would help cancel out the brown," I say as I reach for the appropriate bottle.

Eden lets out an exaggerated sigh. "I'm sick of brown."

I laugh and hand her the blue paint. "Then have at it."

A drop at a time, she adds the color and swirls it with a brush.

As she works, I turn my attention back to my half-finished angel piece from family weekend. I can't decide if I should burn it and the bad vibes of that weekend, build on it, come back to it later, or just start something from scratch.

I still don't connect with this piece—or anything I've been working on lately—so I'm hopeful that when I move outside to the sailboat, it will help spur something creatively.

I grab a piece of paper and roughly sketch the outline of the boat, then make my starting line and continue adding to it.

I glance at the angel piece once again, deciding I am kind of into the ethereal theme and start thinking through the different ways I can depict it. Maybe along the bottom of the boat, I can create wings, then have them come up the sides like they're helping propel the boat forward?

"Do you have a boyfriend?" Eden asks me, breaking our comfortable silence.

I blink in surprise at her question. "What? No."

"What about a girlfriend, then?"

"Not one of those either," I say. "Why are you asking me about this, Eden?"

"I don't know," she tells me, setting the brush down like it's the most precious thing in the world. "Why don't you have one?"

"I had a boyfriend once," I admit, mentally calling up Mike's smiling face in my mind. "It was...nice. But we weren't right for each other."

"Oh," she says softly, looking at me and then at the sketch at my fingertips. "Why isn't Will your boyfriend?"

I choke at her words. "We're just friends, Eden."

She gives me the most skeptical look I've seen on her features. "Really?"

"Really," I say seriously. "Why are you asking me this?"

Eden shrugs. "Just because."

I don't believe her, but I'm not really thrilled about this topic, so I let it go. "Okay."

After a minute of silence, just when I've relaxed back into the drawing, she pipes up again.

"But why do you always paint his scar?" Eden asks.

I'm more startled than I have ever been by her perception—and bluntness.

"What?" I sputter out.

An adorable line creases her forehead as she scrunches up her nose, studying the work in front of me.

"Will's scar," Eden repeats, pointing at the little line that's somewhat hidden by the rest of the drawing. "I saw it in your sketchbook, too. And sometimes you doodle it on the scrap wood."

I'm at a loss for words on how to explain this.

"Is that why he has that tattoo?" Eden presses.

"What?" I balk.

She gives me side-eye. "You know, the one on his chest. Didn't you draw it? It looks like one of yours."

"Will doesn't have a tattoo," I say with sudden uncertainty.

"Yes he does," she says petulantly, tapping just below her collarbone. "Right here."

My breathing is loud in my own ears. "Are you sure?"

"Yeah," she says like I'm an idiot for questioning her.

"Oh," is all I manage.

She, unaware of the grenade she just lobbed in my direction, goes back to staring at the mess of paint that's swirled together.

I remain fixed in momentary shock, wrestling with disbelief while simultaneously believing her words with utmost conviction.

Although little kids definitely have their quirks, they're brutally honest, and I can't imagine Eden would tell me such a wild story if it weren't true.

The session goes on, and the minutes until the campers have to be back at their cabins drag by.

But I can only go through the motions as I count down the time until I can investigate this revelation for myself.

Eden and I add a little more white to the green before resolving to let it dry and see what we think, then I patiently help a camper paint just the right shading on an eyeball to make it come to life.

The moment I'm finally alone, I stride out of the cabin, letting the door slam behind me as I set my sights on the lake.

A few campers wave to me, but once my eyes land on Will, smiling goodbye to one of his assistants as they head up toward the mess hall, I have tunnel vision.

"Will," I call impatiently as I approach.

He's in swim trunks and a life vest, same as he's been in all day. I know this because I may or may not have spent a lot of time watching him unload the kayaks from the art cabin.

But now that I'm armed with Eden's knowledge, I'm not ogling.

I'm searching.

And I'm kind of mad about it.

Especially when he drops his hands from the natural motion he was just starting to do—the unclipping of his life vest.

I've noticed his slight hesitation to do so before, but previously, I assumed it was some sort of modesty thing, his not wanting to be shirtless in my presence.

Now, of course, it makes even more sense.

He's hiding something.

"How's your day?" I ask, covering my anger with a falsely sweet tone.

Will crosses his arms over his chest, immediately picking up on my insincerity. "What's wrong?"

The puffy life vest makes his gesture somewhat comical because, even though half his body is hidden, I can still see the lean muscle and oddly attractive tendons and veins on his arms.

"Nothing," I snap, recalibrating my mind away from how distracting he is.

"Okay, Cameron," he says like I'm the one who is acting a little off.

I put my hands on my hips. "Well?"

"Well what?" Will asks.

"Aren't you going to keep packing up for the night?"

He eyes the disarray of oars just behind me. "Uh, yeah."

I don't move a muscle, slightly blocking his path.

He laughs and runs a hand through his hair, tugging it over the side of his face. "It's kind of odd to do this with you watching me."

"Then I'll help," I offer forcefully.

"Oh, no," he says like it's no big deal. "I've got this."

"Okay."

"You're being weird," Will deflects.

I shake my head. "I'm not being weird."

Will swallows and stares at me head-on, willing me to open up. "Come on, Cameron. Just tell me what's on your mind."

"Take off your life vest," I say simply.

He jolts back in confusion. "What?"

"Take it off."

"Cameron," he says, voice a little rough.

I step forward and don't lose my resolve. "Will."

He squeezes his eyes shut, then opens them again,

likely hoping this confrontation is just some figment of his imagination. "I don't—"

"Want to show me your tattoo?" I interject.

He chews his bottom lip and tilts his head. "You know about that?"

I let out a hollow laugh. "So, it's true?"

Neither of us moves for a beat, remaining frozen in this standoff.

He renews his gaze, locking his eyes with mine as he unclasps both buckles with a *pop!*

I watch his hands shake as he undoes the zipper next, then shrugs off the vest, letting it fall to the ground behind him.

My breath hitches as I step closer, not stopping until my face is mere inches away from the black lines carved into his skin.

I'm looking at one of my early drawings, a depiction of this very view at Camp Creek with the lake and the trees.

Elena was so thrilled that I'd made such a good recovery after the accident and taken to my new hobby that she'd hung the landscape on her refrigerator, and for nearly a decade, it's been in the same spot. It's a little yellowed and frayed on the edges now, but it remains pinned beneath a magnet purchased on some vacation they took years ago.

And it's also permanently marked just below Will's collarbones.

The lines are a little wobbly—the result of my own inexperience, not the tattoo artist's—but it's a perfect rendition.

I don't hesitate to reach out, uncaring that the last time

I touched him resulted in his shutting down and swimming away from me because I'm not letting this one go.

"Will," I say, voice trembling just a bit. "I can't believe this."

I meet his eyes—they're beautiful, dark brown and wide with concern—wondering what he was thinking, then and now.

"How the hell can you tattoo something *permanent* on your body like that?" I demand an answer but my voice has lost every single bit of its venom.

"You seem to like Bellamy's tattoo just fine," Will says in defense.

"That's how you want to play this?" I step back, ensuring he can see my confusion. "Okay. Bellamy asked me to draw something for him specifically, with my consent, to mark his 'foray into adulthood.'"

"I know because I was there when he got it," Will reminds me.

I shake my head. "And you've had months to tell me about yours. But instead, I have to find out from someone else that you have my own art on your skin."

Will studies the ground and digs his toe into the sand.

"Bellamy showed off that tattoo for weeks after he got it," I continue. "But you both conveniently left out any mention of the fact that *you* got something done, too."

"He wasn't there," he admits. "I went back after he got his. I don't even think he knows about mine."

"You guys have been living together, here and at home, for all this time, and you think he doesn't know?" I ask, exasperated.

"I can be pretty stealthy," Will says, biting back a smile.

"You were ratted out to me by an eight-year-old," I remind him.

"Well, regardless, you've always been the observant one."

The chatter between us feels almost normal.

If I close my eyes and block out the ink and the incident last summer, I might be able to pretend it is. But how secretive he's been with this, combined with the mixed signals...

It's too much. Too confusing.

"I just—" I hate how my voice breaks, so I swallow before I start speaking again. "I don't understand, Will."

All the lightness evaporates from his demeanor as his shoulders slump and jaw tightens, and the ease is gone just as soon as it came over us.

I try to channel all the boldness I've observed in Tori and project that myself, but I got shut down by Will once already. It's going to take everything in me to stay strong in case it happens again.

I take a breath before I begin. "When I tried to tell you last summer how I felt, you stated, very clearly, that you weren't interested in anything more than—"

"Come on, Cameron," he interrupts, backing away.

"No," I snap as I take a step. "We are going to talk about this."

He stops, surprised by my tone, I think, and I watch his mouth form a hard line.

But he says nothing.

"You don't want to be with me romantically," I say, pretending those words don't gut me. "But you feel strongly enough toward me that you got something I drew tattooed on you? Help me understand this."

I give him a minute to stare at me and awkwardly fidget while I wait calmly for some sort of explanation.

"You're the best person I know, Cameron," he says finally.

Fighting the immediate urge to respond, I keep quiet, waiting to see what else he offers.

"You're so brilliant, so beautiful, so talented…"

My heart swells in my chest.

"And you give so much of yourself to other people. Not just to me, but Bellamy, our families, now Tori, anyone who needs it." He pauses and tugs at the ends of his hair. "You can't keep taking care of people all the time."

"I'm not following," I admit to him.

"Take me, for example." Will's hand flits to his chest, briefly covering the artwork that started this entire conversation. "You worry about me constantly."

I balk at that accusation, but he goes on before I can open my mouth.

"You are livid at every single person who even thinks about my scar the wrong way, and you're always checking in on how I'm feeling…it's constant."

"Is something wrong with me wanting you to be okay?" I ask seriously.

"No, of course not," Will says quickly. "I just don't need you to keep reminding me of what happened, tying us to that freak accident, and feeling bad about it. I mean, it happened so long ago."

"This isn't really about me, then, is it? Your concern for my mental and emotional capacity." I huff in irritation. "It's about *you*. How you've never come to terms with anything, so you want to push me away because I make you feel something."

Will smiles sadly. "I just want you to see me the way you see everyone else."

"How the hell can I do that, Will? I've been in love with you since I was four years old, so of course I'm going to look at you differently!"

I don't even process the words that have come from my mouth until I take in the look of complete and utter panic on his face.

I sigh and cross my arms on my chest. "Forget it."

"Cameron."

"It's fine," I say in a clipped tone. "You've told me no before, that you'd just rather be friends, and I'd really rather not hear it again."

He frowns in confusion. "You *still* feel this way about me?"

I drop my gaze, and gravity or defiance gives way for the tears to roll down my cheeks. I shake my head as I wipe away my tears, feeling silly for so many reasons.

"You have to understand, Cameron," Will says quickly. "At the time, I didn't want—"

"Will," I say, squeezing my eyes shut briefly. "Please don't. I'm begging you to not say anything else about this."

I take a breath in silence before I meet his gaze, and the look of pity he's giving me makes me want to bury myself in the sand.

"Cameron," Will mutters, reaching for me.

"We *are* better as friends," I say, stepping back and trying to end this conversation with a shred of dignity.

"And I'm…flattered that you got the tattoo. We only have a few weeks left together, Will. You, me, and Bellamy. I don't want this to be weird."

Will runs a hand through his hair and lets out a breath. "If that's what you want."

"It is."

"Okay," he says quietly.

I'm grateful for his assent, but I can tell it's still on his mind.

I take a second to bat away any residual tears before I clear my throat and plaster on a smile. "So, are you done patching the hole in the boat?"

It takes him a second to follow me onto the new topic. "Yeah," he says with a nod. "I finished it the other day."

"Good," I say resolutely. "I'm ready to get to work."

Because while I might be smothering my true feelings for him, I might as well use my inner turmoil to fuel my art.

TWELVE

"You're going to break that piece of paper," Tori warns.

The door slams behind her as she crosses the small distance to the side of my bed, then sits unceremoniously on top of it.

I lessen my grip on the block of charcoal, and the relief on my fingers is instant.

I didn't realize I was holding it so tightly or pressing it that fiercely against the paper, but it explains why there is far more black than white smudged on the page.

"It feels like you've been wound a little tightly all week," Tori says with a frown.

"Yeah, well..." I stop when I realize I don't have anything to add.

But I finally glance up, realizing that the sun has been set for a while—and dinner ended hours ago.

Judging by the way her hair is mussed and the lipstick she borrowed from me is a little smeared at the corner, it's obvious that Bellamy's to blame for her absence.

It's very much frowned upon for counselors and crew members to miss curfew, but she regularly breaks it. Matthew insists it sets a bad example for the campers, but I think he just loves the control and telling people what to do.

"This is the closest I've seen you get to the 'tortured artist' trope," she says, tone teasing.

I shrug and drop my gaze back to my sketchbook, making no effort to engage in conversation.

"And I think, really, the only thing to do in these circumstances of whatever you're feeling but refuse to discuss is go out and blow off some steam," Tori says.

I look up, giving her my full attention. "What?"

"Before you come up with excuses about rule-breaking, let me say I've gotten it all taken care of." Tori smiles in a way that's almost excessively smug, eyebrows raised and the corner of her mouth hitched up. "Brody owes me."

"For what?"

"I distracted Rebecca a few weeks ago when she was on the brink of finding his and Caitlin's secret hookup spot." Tori is almost too proud to share this information. "So he's going to take us to our destination tonight, be our designated driver. And he will take your shift tomorrow morning."

She swipes my cosmetic bag and mirror from the shelf and drops it between us, signaling that it's time to get a move on. "Don't smack a gift horse in the mouth."

"Are you serious?" I ask as she fixes and reapplies her lipstick.

"Deadly," she intones.

I chew on my bottom lip, trying to decide if it's even worth putting up a fight.

When we went out earlier in the summer, I went from feeling like an outsider to having a blast in just the span of a few hours, and I'm not sure if I'm up for that roller-coaster tonight.

I squeeze the sketchbook in my hands, then stare at my creation.

It's a somewhat ambiguous person depicted across a few cracked mirrors. I don't feel any connection to it. Despite my best efforts, I'm just as unenthused by this piece as the last few I've drawn.

Would I really be better off if I stay here?

"Come on," Tori chides. "I think you could use a break."

I sigh and relent, knowing that with her persistence I'd give in eventually. "How long do we have to get ready?"

She laughs and claps her hands. "Yes! As long as it takes."

We decide to go all-out for our outfits and makeup.

I feel a little looser and more relaxed as Tori sings along horribly to the music playing from her phone. She gives me free rein to do her eyeshadow and eyeliner, then talks me into creating an equally dramatic look for myself.

I don't hesitate to put on the crop top she hands over, and by the time we reach Brody's car, we're both drunk on the excitement of sneaking out and the anticipation for what the night might hold.

It's a little after nine, which seems very late in the context of Camp Creek but is when the bar just starts to ramp up, apparently.

"Ladies," Brody waves us through the entryway.

"Thank you, kind sir," Tori returns.

She and I step past him with our arms linked, like we're two women about to destroy all of our foes and take over the world.

Our reality isn't that dramatic, though, because we merely join up with a group of male counselors who have also snuck out.

They're sharing a tale with a few guys I don't recognize, and they all greet one another with that handshake-slash-one-arm-over-the-shoulder hug.

"I thought it was just the three of us," I murmur to Tori.

"Did I say that?" she says innocently.

"Tori," I warn as I dig my fingertips in her arm, trying to bring her to a halt.

She groans, putting on an exaggerated display of frustration by throwing her head back before she widens her eyes at me. "Cameron."

"Tori," I return evenly.

"Am I going to have to give you a pep talk for every social interaction that's not with the Moreno twins? You deserve a night out. Just try and hold onto the excitement you had five minutes ago when we were dancing in Brody's car. Just because the setting has changed and there are more people than you were expecting doesn't mean you have to clam up." She squeezes my side, making me laugh involuntarily. "Don't you agree, Brody?"

"Absolutely," he says with confidence. "Come on, I'll introduce you."

"I'm a *fantastic* wingwoman," Tori insists as we move.

I exhale. "Great."

"Don't look down," she coaches, tapping on the edge of

my jaw. "That's the first sign of weakness. Don't ever walk into a room with any attitude other than you own the place. Keep your shoulders back, scan the crowd, then smile at whoever catches your interest."

Somehow, I find it easy to follow her instructions.

I slide into the space between her and Brody, who both make a show of introducing me to the unfamiliar faces as "an artist." I suppose the label gives me some air of mystery, and I kind of love it.

Tori pushes the conversation forward, and I focus on just trying to enjoy the experience, which is nice but kind of a strange one for me.

In school, I was always hanging around with Bellamy, Will, and some of our mutual friends. After years of growing up together, my personality was fixed, built on years of inside jokes, shared classes, and stories from Camp Creek.

But I get somewhat of a blank slate here.

Which is why I finally award that smile Tori insisted I project to a guy named Dan who's been trying to catch my eye for the past twenty minutes.

"So, Cameron," he says, angling his body toward mine.

It's not a stance that crowds me, exactly, but I think it's an intentional signal to the rest of the table that he's trying to break us apart from them.

I take a sip from my water glass. "So, Dan."

"Good start," he says. "You know my name."

He smiles widely, and by the way the gesture cuts deep lines around his eyes and shows off his dimples, I can tell it's given easily—and regularly.

There's no brooding, no shying away or hiding from his feelings.

I find it absurdly refreshing.

"Well, it's not that difficult to remember," I tell him. "Three letters. One syllable. No fuss."

"That's me in a nutshell," Dan jokes.

I bite the corner of my lip. "I suppose brevity's not the worst character trait."

"And what's the *best* character trait, according to you?"

"Well, I'm no expert, but I do have some thoughts," I say, feigning deep consideration.

"I'd love to hear them."

I tilt my head, trying to assess if he's genuinely interested in what I think or just flirting with me for the hell of it.

In my peripheral vision, I catch Tori's excited gaze flicking between us, no doubt just as eager to watch this happen in real-time as she will be to dissect it when we're alone later.

"Hit me with them," Dan insists. "You and your three syllables must have a lot of perspective."

I toss my hair over my shoulder, then tick off on my fingers, "Compassion. Honesty. Integrity." I stop and let out a chuckle. "God, I sound like a slogan for an insurance company."

He shakes his head. "I think those are all admirable traits in a person."

Brody's voice carries over us as he asks the group, "Anyone up for karaoke?"

His question is met with various groans—with one exception.

"Hell yes," Tori says enthusiastically. "I think they're starting a line over there."

She then moves on instinct, I think, to pull me along with her, but at the last second slips her arm through Brody's instead.

I watch the two of them walk away, leaving me to fend for myself.

"Not one for karaoke?" Dan asks me.

He's re-engaging our conversation when he easily could have turned his attention back to his friends, and the realization thrills me just a little bit.

"Hearing me sing would be a punishment," I say lightly.

He shakes his head. "I doubt it would be a worse one than hearing me."

"Then let's make a promise to never find out."

"Probably for the best. I'm trying to make a good impression on you, not prove why I got kicked out of chorus in middle school."

I laugh at his self-deprecation. "In our school, I'm pretty sure everyone who signed up could be in it."

"Mine, too," he tells me. "That's why it's even worse that I got asked to leave."

"Ouch," I say with a grin. "Dreams dashed at such a young age. Have you recovered?"

"I like to think so, but maybe my resentment is swirling around in some deep-rooted issues that'll surface in some way in the future."

I quirk a brow as I take another sip of water.

"Sorry," he says. "I'm a psych major."

"Major? You're already in college?"

"Yeah. I'm heading up early next week, actually. I've got

an apartment with some of these guys." He gestures vaguely to the dudes who are in some sort of heated argument over baseball teams. "You're going to be a freshman, right?"

"Yes."

"Well, as an older, wiser, much more experienced, rising sophomore, I'm at your disposal. You can ask me for all the tips and tricks."

"Oh?" I ask, feigning skepticism. "And what words of wisdom do you have for me?"

"Show compassion." He taps his fingers on the table. "Be honest. Have integrity."

It takes me a beat to realize he's teasing me about my earlier character traits, then I let out a genuine laugh before I roll my eyes.

"I'm kidding," he says before amending his statement. "Actually, I don't think any of those would hurt."

"I want real advice," I tell him haughtily, crossing my arms over my chest.

He twists his lips to the side. "Are you living in the dorms?"

"Uh-huh. I should hear who my roommate is when I get home."

"Good luck with that," he says ominously. "You're going to need it."

"Something tells me you're projecting a bad experience onto me. Maybe my roommate is some fabulous person I'll get along with really well. Or some billionaire's daughter who wants to buy me really expensive gifts and have catered meals all the time."

He chuckles. "More like someone who will eat the last

of your best snacks and 'forget' that it wasn't a communal offering."

"See?" I say, waving my hand his way. "Projecting."

"Okay, okay, fine," he admits.

As I smile, I realize this is the experience that I, an eighteen-year-old with no romantic attachments, should be having right now. Silly banter about mundane things, a way to feel out the other person before opening up to something deeper.

This is how it starts, really.

Testing the waters on compatibility. One discussion is supposed to lead to another, then we'll spend hours getting to know each other. A little shy and awkward at first, but over time, things that once excited us will become normal.

At least, that's how it happened with my ex-boyfriend.

Mike and I sat across the table from each other in study hall, and after a few weeks of catching each other's gaze, I struck up a conversation with him.

We had to speak in low tones, but we started commiserating over our mutual hatred of our anatomy class.

He then asked for my number, and while we stuck to school-related texting conversations at first, our relationship began to build.

I found his easygoing attitude and intelligence charming, and it was almost easy to start spending time together after school.

It was like we had a list with things to check off—first date, first kiss, first school dance, first holidays, first... everything else.

We did all the things couples were supposed to do, but

for as much as I wanted to fall for him completely, it felt like something was missing.

I don't know if he and I just weren't compatible or if I was just going to continue being a lost cause for Will.

I renew my gaze on Dan, trying to imagine if it'll be like that with him.

I could be brave enough to initiate the innocent contact between us—maybe a graze of my knuckles on his, opening up the invitation for him to move closer, slide his arm around my back.

We'll start exploring each other, emotionally and physically, and a relationship will grow from there.

The thought of being touched and loved makes the lonely part of my heart throb, but it still feels off, somehow, as I look at him.

"...and when I took them out of the dryer," Dan continues, "I realized not only had I stained all my shirts pink, but they'd all shrunk at least a size and a half."

"Dan," I say suddenly, reaching for his hand.

His fingers immediately tangle in mine. "Cameron."

A dangerous idea is forming, and I'm not sure if I should go with it.

Tori would encourage me if she was here and not arguing with Brody on the other side of the bar, so I do.

"Do you want to go get some air?" I blurt out.

He gives me that lovely smile again. "Sure."

I see how Tori eyes me curiously as Dan and I leave through the propped-open door, and I nod to her, signaling that I'm fine, then she turns to whisper something to Brody.

"Is this enough air for you?" Dan asks, amused as he glances around.

We come to a stop at the edge of the parking lot. It's just far enough from the lights of the building that they lend a gentle hue to his features while we stand a little hidden away.

It's definitely not the most romantic of settings, but it'll do.

"So, what do you think you're going to major—"

"Dan," I interject. "We've done enough talking."

He blinks, startled by my boldness.

In truth, I am as well because this is ridiculously out of character for me.

I mean, the whole night is, starting from the moment I agreed to come, down to what I look like and what I'm doing.

But I feel charged up and determined—two traits that are also a rarity for me—so I cling to them like they're a life vest.

A life *raft*, I mean.

Not a vest like the one that's regularly pressed up against Will's tattooed chest.

I shake those thoughts away.

"Is it okay if I kiss you?" I ask Dan, earning my widest grin yet.

"Yes," he says simply.

He takes a step toward me, his eyes narrowed with intrigue as his hands, which are lovely and warm and rough, hit the exposed skin of my waist.

I put my hand on his chest as he starts to lean down. "Before we do this, I have a confession."

"What?" His tone is quiet but forceful and deep at the same time.

"You're a test," I admit.

He tilts his head to the side. "A test?"

"Yes," I say evenly, not losing my resolve. "I think there's chemistry between us."

"Oh, there definitely is."

I laugh, breaking the spell of seriousness just a bit before I double down. "There's…someone else. And I'm not sure if I'm just clinging to you to get over him."

He seems almost amused by the idea. "You're using me?"

"Well, not exactly," I say quickly. "I mean, I think you're great. At least, that's the opinion I've formed in the hour or so I've known you. But I don't know, like, what the expectations are with this. I thought if I just went for it without this context, it could be misleading, and then I'd have trouble sleeping until I apologized, so I figured I'd clarify."

"Cameron," Dan says slowly, emphasizing those three syllables we talked about.

My chest rises and falls rapidly. "Dan."

"I don't care about the circumstances. I think I'm just going to kiss you now because we don't need any more talking."

"No more talking," I agree.

I stand up on my tiptoes and lock my arms around his neck, pulling him in.

He obliges immediately and leans down to kiss me.

There definitely are sparks.

My heart pounds, and the movement is good, so I concentrate on the rhythm as his hands tangle in my hair.

It's not all-encompassing, though, like it doesn't fill some void in my chest cavity as we rock together.

But when his tongue parts my lips, I lose myself just a bit.

He pulls back, too soon in my opinion, and a dreamy grin forms as he opens his eyes.

"Well?" Dan prompts, gaze flicking between my mouth and my eyes.

He's close enough that if I pressed upward, we'd kiss again, and I think I want to do it.

I clear my throat. "Th-thank you."

He chuckles and brushes a lock of hair away from my face. "Not the reaction I was looking for."

I drop my gaze to the ground. "It was nice."

Dan lets out a choking laugh and presses his hand to his chest like I've wounded him.

"I'm so sorry," I say with a wince.

I move to pull out of his embrace, but he holds me tight, then tilts my head up with his thumb.

"It's fine, Cameron," Dan says reassuringly. "I agreed to this, remember? As much as I'm enjoying getting to know you, I don't think my heart is shattered."

"Maybe this is a good thing, then, because I think your ego needs a hit," I say with a laugh.

"Maybe," he allows. "Let's find out."

And then he kisses me again.

THIRTEEN

I had a really great time last night, Cameron.

Me too. :)

Let me know if you ever need another test subject…

I can't help but beam at the words Dan texts me.

"What's got you smiling so big?" Tori asks me as she sits down beside Will.

"Nothing," I say innocently.

"Well, it certainly can't be this staff meeting," she breathes, making a big show of her exasperation.

I make a noncommittal noise in my throat as I shove my phone in my pocket.

Will eyes me curiously, a little line forming on his forehead as he assesses my mood.

My happiness is definitely an improvement over all the moping around I've been doing the past week, pretending that I'm perfectly fine pouring my heart out to him and then frantically shoving my feelings back inside.

"Was it *Dan*?" Tori asks, emphasizing his name in speed and sound.

Will's gaze moves between my flat expression and Tori's devilishly happy one. "Who's Dan?"

"This guy Cameron met last night," she supplies before closing her mouth tightly, leaving the words hanging between us.

I don't take the bait to fill in the details, though, because I know exactly what Tori's doing.

And while I admire many of her traits, this isn't one of them.

I'm not in the mood to play games with anyone—now or ever—and I don't need to try to make Will jealous.

It's not like he's going to have a sudden burst of feelings for me.

And even if he did miraculously change his mind, it would be really crappy if this was a catalyst for something so life-altering.

This is why I was so straightforward with him a year ago—hell, even days ago—and the same with Dan last night.

Life is complicated enough without all this extra nonsense.

Most of all, though, deception is not worth the attempted effort, so I go for blunt honesty.

"We went out last night," I explain to Will. "Brody, Tori, me. There were a few counselors there, and they had some friends in town. We met a few guys who are going to the Penn State branch about an hour from here in the fall."

"Oh," Will says evenly. "Cool."

"Tori and Brody took charge of the karaoke this time," I continue, giving him more details than he's probably interested in. "Spice Girls was their group of choice."

"Not that you would know," Tori says a little smugly before addressing Will directly. "She and Dan disappeared for most of my performance."

"Tori," I warn as I shake my head.

Will shifts in his seat in discomfort. "What about your shift this morning? I've never known you to be able to go out and function the next day on a lack of sleep."

"So nice and *friendly* of you to have Cameron's schedule memorized," Tori says pointedly.

"Brody covered it for me," I tell him.

I can't decipher any emotion on Will's face, and it's not a good feeling.

"Cool," he says evenly.

Tori's posture slumps, and she shakes her head in exasperation, evidently irritated by the lack of reaction from either of us.

But just because I don't show it doesn't mean I don't feel it.

I know it will take time for me to continue getting over Will, and as much as I'm devastated for him, Bellamy, and me to go to separate schools in the fall, part of me wonders if it's needed.

Change is scary, but I think it's also going to be necessary.

Last night's...event with Dan served as a good reminder that there are other people out there—not just romantic interests, but even as friends.

As much as I've clung to the Morenos, furthering my independence and finding myself is probably what's right at this stage in my life.

And I'm starting to really look forward to it.

"Hello, everyone," Rebecca calls.

She's greeted with a few half-hearted hellos.

"This summer is flying by, isn't it?" Rebecca continues.

"Yes," Matthew says as he steps forward. "And we still have a lot of work to do."

"We are so proud of how smoothly things have been running so far."

Matthew glares around the room. "But now's not the time to slack off just because the end is in sight."

"I hate that guy," Bellamy whispers as he takes the seat beside me.

I smile at him, instantly relaxing in his presence and wondering if he had some sort of best friend sense that I needed comforting.

Bellamy offers me a half-smile and a wink, then reaches over to squeeze my hand.

"Who's excited for the overnight trips this week?" Rebecca asks enthusiastically.

The counselors in attendance are the loudest with their claps and hollers. I can only assume at this point in the summer, they're ready for new scenery away from their cabins.

From what I recall, there are a bunch of different options, like whitewater rafting, backpacking, kayaking, and rock climbing—all outdoorsy stuff.

It's only one night over sleeping in a tent, but I barely managed to suffer through it as a camper—I couldn't imagine having to give up the comfort of my pillows and reinforced mattress now.

"But we do have some change-ups in the assignments," Matthew announces. "Many of you haven't heard, but Caitlin's come down with the flu and is holed up in the clinic for the next few days."

A murmur of sympathy ripples through the room, but Bellamy chuckles under his breath.

"I was in there yesterday for my vitamin T, and she's absolutely faking it," he whispers.

"Really?" I ask.

"I mean, who wouldn't want to get out of hiking with a bunch of bratty kids?"

"So, we're moving things around," Matthew continues. "We're hoping to figure out how to cover all the trips without causing too much disruption to everyone else's normal schedule."

"Yes," Rebecca takes over. "We're asking any willing crew members to step in. A few of you are already in the rotation, but we need one more person to volunteer for Caitlin's spot on the caving trip."

"I'll do it," Tori offers.

Rebecca glances at her clipboard. "But you're signed on for the kayak trip with Will."

"Right," Tori confirms, then offers her biggest smile. "But it makes more sense for me to step into the caving trip, as my regular program has absolutely nothing to do with water."

"That's fair," Rebecca admits. "But I'll still need a volunteer to—"

"Cameron can do it," Tori says, nudging me with her

elbow.

I glare at her before I turn to Rebecca. "I'm sure someone else would be more capable."

"No, no." Her eyes light up in response. "If we can slide you in that slot, then we won't have to move anyone else."

"I'll actually be pretty busy here, helping the older campers with their final pieces," I argue with a smile.

"We can just give the campers extra time in the rec area instead of the arts cabin," she decides.

Matthew claps his hands. "Great."

I grit my teeth, refusing to look in the direction of Will or Tori as I come to terms with what this means—not just the physical activity but just being in the close proximity of Will for nearly twenty-four hours straight as we attempt to wrangle a group of kids.

"Please be ready by seven o'clock on the morning of your trip," Matthew concludes after a few more announcements. "All supplies will be loaded in the vans for you, and we'll coordinate a seamless exit."

"Thanks again, everyone," Rebecca says brightly. "Meeting adjourned!"

I let out a massive sigh and stand immediately to get away from here, but before I go, Bellamy reaches for my arm.

He tugs me to the side. "Can you stick around for a bit?"

"Of course," I say immediately, following his lead away from the others.

I keep my eyes locked on the back of his skull as we cross behind the counter.

The kitchen is surprisingly empty for this time of day,

but we still don't come to a stop until we reach the far back corner, away from stragglers from the meeting and tucked away behind some shelves.

Bellamy double-checks that we're alone before he turns to me. "Are you okay?"

"Yeah," I tell him, only a little weary. "I'm okay."

"Good," he says with a breath of relief. "I heard you went out last night, and I wasn't sure how you were faring."

I shake my head. "What exactly did Tori tell you?"

"She went with you?" He stops, and a look of understanding dawns on him. "Of course. Why else would you voluntarily hang out with Brody, of all people?"

"Hey, now," I deflect. "I like Brody. He's nice. And so is Caitlin."

Bellamy snorts. "Even though her fake illness means you now have to spend two days kayaking?"

It's not the kayaking I'm dreading so much as all that time with Will.

That's not something I ever thought possible, but after our conversation and my only slightly successful test last night with Dan, I could use a break and some alone time.

And this is the opposite of that.

"I guess," I say after a beat.

"Liar," Bellamy teases.

I rub my temples. "I kissed someone last night."

His jaw drops. "What? Who? And how was it?"

"Actually, you know, I really shouldn't be sharing this with you," I backpedal. "Weren't you saying something a few weeks ago about not kissing and telling?"

"That was old me," he says flippantly. "New me is a bundle of love and joy and oversharing."

He tries to suppress the smile on his face, but his elation is too powerful.

"Bellamy," I say slowly. "What'd you do?"

He fishes his wallet from his back pocket, then hands it over. "It's not what I did but what has happened."

I take it from his outstretched hand. "Okay?"

"Open it," he urges with a chuckle.

I run my thumb over the worn leather billfold I got him for Christmas two years ago, checking the cash within, then tap his cards—and let out a gasp.

"Bellamy," I breathe.

My heart pounds and glee overtakes every other emotion as I slide his license out of its protective sleeve.

"You didn't tell me it was coming!"

"I didn't know," he says honestly.

I lift the little rectangle of plastic to get a closer look. "Bellamy."

"I've been through Pennsylvania's bureaucratic hell for weeks. My parents overnighted it to me when it arrived, so I just got it yesterday."

"Look at that," I say, my voice breaking slightly as I trace the gender marker, now designated with an M.

"Don't get all soft on me, Cameron," Bellamy says, even as he's a little teary-eyed.

All my problems seem so trivial compared to the pride, joy, and love I feel for this man standing before me.

I reach out to hug him, and he pulls me in for a tight embrace.

"I love you so much," I murmur.

"I love you, too," he says before kissing the top of my head.

We stay like that, a collective mess of tears and emotions, until the bustle of dinner prep begins.

FOURTEEN

The day starts off fine enough.

I arrive at the van on time, as do Will and most of the campers.

He does a final check of the gear that's been packed for us as I take quick attendance of the kids joining us. They seem to be excited, even if a little tired at this earlier hour.

The old radio in the van is out, so for the duration of the hour-and-a-half drive up toward the river, we're subjected to repetitive camp songs and incessant adolescent chatter.

When we finally arrive at the parking area by the water, the kids practically burst out of the confinement.

It's an overcast day, but Will still lectures everyone about putting on sunscreen as we unload the little yellow boats. We each are responsible for carrying our own bags and helping to set up camp—if we make it there.

"I'll tow the extra kayak with the tent supplies," Will

tells me as some of the campers start wading into the water.

It's the longest string of words either of us has put together until now.

"Okay," I say, dragging the remaining kayak out of the trailer.

"Life vest," Will calls before I enter the water.

I sigh as I double back, taking it from his outstretched fingertips.

"Safety first," he says smartly.

"Uh-huh," I breathe as I slip it on, ignoring his direct gaze.

The day carries on as expected, and we all move along the relatively placid river.

Several of the campers get caught up in goofing off instead of rowing along, and Will has to pull one frustrated kid aside to give him a stern talking-to about bringing down the morale of the group.

Even at our leisurely pace, my arms are already burning by the time we pull over for lunch.

It's a very glamorous meal of prepacked sandwiches and granola bars, which we all scarf down fairly quickly, then get back on the water and resume our offbeat rowing.

I'm so focused on the proper form and not falling too far behind that I ignore the sprinkles of rain.

If anything, they're a welcome coolant to combat the physical exertion, but as the rain picks up in severity and the water surface gets a little choppy, Will voices his concern.

"I think we should pull over early," Will says, paddling a little extra fiercely to catch up to me.

He's been mostly hanging back, ensuring that no one gets left behind.

I've been grateful for it because the way the fabric of his shirt clings to his muscles is a very big distraction from the beauty around us.

"That sounds fine," I say casually.

I'm doing a great job of pretending like I'm not screaming a celebration inside my brain—I can already feel the blisters forming on my hands.

"There's a campsite up ahead," he tells me as he checks the paper map. "It's not as nice as the one I had planned, but it'll do."

I'm trying not to reveal how breathless I am from rowing. "Sounds good."

"Do you mind staying at the back? I'm going to head up front to corral the group to the right spot."

"Go ahead," I grit out.

He stops rowing to glance at me.

And frustratingly enough, he still moves at the same speed I'm paddling along.

"Are you okay?" Will asks.

I keep my gaze forward. "Yes."

He doesn't say anything, merely watching me for a minute before he starts up again, easily closing the distance from where I am to the front of the group.

When I eventually make it to shore, the group is already unpacking—and getting increasingly rowdy.

The girls have their six-person tent set up, and the boys are arguing and laughing as they try to fix how slanted theirs is.

Will just looks plain exasperated, hair a mess of twists

and eyes tight with concern as a rain drop plops on the middle of his forehead.

I drag my kayak over by the others, then unceremoniously toss my life vest aside before joining everyone.

By the time I've stretched and secured my bag, the campers are getting into their tents, shedding their soaked gear and rolling out their sleeping bags, making it clear they're ready to pass out.

I'm eager to crawl into my own space and do the same.

"There's only one adult tent," Will tells me evenly as rain drips down his nose.

"What?" I take in the four round bags at his feet. "Those aren't for us?"

"They are, but instead of two sleeping bags and two tents, they mistakenly gave us *three* sleeping bags and one tent."

I sigh as he pulls the very singular tent out of the bag.

"I can try and squeeze in with the girls," I offer.

He shakes his head. "Both tents are packed already, and it's got everyone on edge. I had to settle an argument while you were coming up."

"Oh," I say, eyeing our tight sleeping quarters that Will begins to set up. "Do you want some help?"

"I've got it."

He moves quickly, putting together the space in what I assume is record time—it might just look more complicated to me than it is—then shoves the remaining gear inside.

"Well, we've been sharing forts since we were kids, so I'm sure it'll be fine," I say, reassuring myself more than him, I'm sure.

He holds open the flap for me, and I all but dive in, kicking my shoes off close to the entrance.

"I'll be right back," he says.

While he's off checking on the others, I set up a cozy nest of our sleeping bags, trying to leave a clear line between the two sides.

It's kind of ridiculous, though, because I'm pretty sure that this tent is actually intended for one child-size occupant, not two adults. We're both going to have to sleep on our sides just to avoid touching each other.

A roll of thunder rumbles in the distance, causing the girls to shriek over the now almost downpour occurring outside.

"Everyone's fine," Will announces upon his return, water dripping from the ends of his hair.

I peek out at our surroundings, letting out a breath of relief that we're high enough to abate any risk of flooding, meaning Will picked a good placc to sct up camp.

I don't compliment him, though, choosing instead to pull my phone out of the waterproof bag. There are two missed calls from my sister, but my phone hovers between one bar and no service—not that I would return her call, anyway.

I exchange the useless device for the tank top and sleep shorts I haphazardly packed this morning, laying them out with a frown.

I expected a night of indulging in s'mores, then crawling into my tent—alone—and sleeping with the vent open to take in the stars.

Now, though, with my sopping wet clothes and hair, I feel chilled to the bone.

I shiver as I turn to Will, who has apparently been watching me with a look of contemplation on his face.

"Can you turn away so I can change?" I ask.

He nods as he pulls out a new pair of basketball shorts for himself. "I, um, don't have an extra shirt," he says carefully.

I pretend the visual of his bare chest doesn't warm my entire body by ten degrees. "That's fine."

I'm surprised my voice doesn't betray my inner thoughts.

We shift around, bumping elbows as we turn away and slip out of our rain-soaked apparel, then I hastily braid my hair.

"You good?" Will asks after a few minutes.

"Yeah," I say as I secure the elastic.

I then lay out my soaked shorts and shirt, knowing there's no chance in hell they'll be dry by morning—but hoping nonetheless.

He does the same, then rifles through a plastic bag to pull out s'mores ingredients.

"At least there's chocolate," I sigh, reaching for a bar.

"I have Skittles, too," he says before tossing a little pack over his shoulder.

I actually manage to catch it. "Thank you. Bellamy's a saint."

"Right," Will says a little coolly.

He focuses on unpacking and sorting through the supplies we have left, so I take out my drawing materials. I only brought a few worn-down pencils and a sharpie, figuring I wouldn't have time to do much more than capture little sights and scenes on our short, busy trip.

I sit back to stretch out my legs, pop a few candies in my mouth, and open the sketchbook on my lap.

Will flips on a little battery-powered lantern. "Here we go."

"Nice," I say.

"Now we have..." He trails off as he finally turns and takes me in.

The expression on his face does wonderful and terrible things to my heart.

It's all the more effective because I have a completely unobscured view of him with his hair swept back, showing off the slight curve of his mouth and darkening of his eyes.

I can't recall a time I've ever been on the receiving end of this type of gaze from him.

And it takes me a good amount of time to associate words with what I'm seeing—shock, desire, longing.

I swallow and self-consciously scratch at the lacy straps of my tank top.

Will remains still, averting his gaze after he comes out of whatever the hell he's thinking about to feel embarrassed for staring.

Finally, he clears his throat. "I can't believe this weather."

Small talk about the outdoors is not what I expected to come out of his mouth, and all I can do is let out a little hum of agreement.

I fix my gaze on the wall of the tent, where I can see little droplets splatter on the outside of the material that the tent is made from.

"We're at a higher elevation than Camp Creek, right?" I ask eventually to restart the conversation, desperately needing to have some sound that's not just the steady rain.

"Yeah, so we should be in for a slightly easier paddle back tomorrow," Will answers. "As long as this clears out by morning."

"Okay," I say quietly.

I'm so conscious of every single movement both of us make that I feel like it's almost a delicate atmosphere between us.

Will nudges the s'mores fixings with his knuckles. "Hungry?"

"Always," I tell him with a small smile.

"What'll it be, then? A s'more or a peanut butter sandwich?"

I set my drawing materials aside and scoot closer to him. "A hybrid," I decide immediately.

"A hybrid?" Will repeats.

"Trust the process," I say confidently.

I open one of the little bags containing a premade sandwich. I gently pull apart the slices of bread, then crumble a graham cracker over the peanut butter smear.

Once satisfied with a generous coating, I break up the chocolate as best I can into small pieces, then arrange them neatly on top of my creation like some sort of mosaic.

"Only you can make art out of this kind of thing," Will says with adoration.

I only hope it's dim enough in here that he can't see me blush.

The marshmallows come next. They prove to be a challenge with no utensils, but I make it work, even if every single one of my fingers is sticky as a result.

Once I'm satisfied, I smash the two pieces of bread back together, then proudly hold up my creation for him to see.

"Impressive," Will says, tone light as he reaches for a plain, boring sandwich of his own.

"Now the test," I tell him before I sink my teeth in.

I have to stop myself from moaning in pleasure at how delicious my mad creation is.

The mixture of the crunchiness from the graham cracker and the softness of the bread, combined with the divinity of the chocolate and extra sweetness of the marshmallow…

I swallow a bite, not without some effort, then gush.

"This is the best thing I've ever had in my life." I take another, then, around my mouthful, add, "You *have* to try this."

His expression is playful at my glee.

I hold the sandwich up for him, expecting him to hold it in his own hands, but he simply leans forward and takes a bite, right over mine, leaving teeth marks in the bread.

"Not bad," he admits after he swallows.

"I question your taste," I tease.

We sit in contemplative silence for a moment as we take in the much-needed calories—even if it's mostly just fat and sugar.

My eyes wander to the little tattoo on his chest, and despite this entire situation being somewhat of a disaster, I've never been more grateful for rain and lack of foresight in packing until this moment.

Tori is going to *love* this entire situation when I tell her about it tomorrow.

"It's already happening," Will says quietly.

I meet his eyes, jolted from my thoughts and curious for a window into his. "What is?"

"We're changing."

I can't help but internally laugh as I compare my line of thinking to his—me being lust-driven and him being contemplative.

"Yes," I say after I swallow the last bite. "We are."

Will brushes the back of his hand against his lips. "I knew that would happen in the fall, obviously, but I thought...just one final summer would be manageable."

"What does that mean?" I ask him to clarify.

He drops his gaze briefly, then meets my eyes.

This version of him, features clear and bright and a little sad, is something I'm going to remember for the rest of my life.

"Everything I said to you by the lake is true, Cameron." He sucks his bottom lip between his teeth, pinning it down like he's trying to hold the words in. "Each and every single day, your talent, your determination, your intelligence...I'm awed by you."

He's being devastatingly serious, but I'm so rocked by this declaration that I let out a strained chuckle.

It's a defense mechanism, or maybe a coping one, but I let it out.

"You can't just say things like that, Will. Make some grand declaration and then expect me to be an emotionless human being about it." I cross my arms over my chest. "You're being cruel."

"I don't want to be."

Will's tone is quiet and almost pained, and he wrings

his hands, then inhales like he's preparing to let out some sort of devastating news.

"I don't want to be cruel or standoffish or in denial anymore. I just want..."

My breath hitches in my throat.

Before I can fully register what he's even saying, he's on the move.

His hands slide up my arms, skim gently over my collarbones, then up to cup the sides of my face. His touch makes me feel more alive than any moment I spent with Mike or Dan or anyone else on the planet.

It's all I can do to try to memorize the experience as his lips meet mine.

My heart wants to explode with excitement and passion and fury, but my mind is logical, wondering what this all means.

Is this a reaction to me going out the other night? Or am I, in some way, a test for him, too? Maybe this is his way of saying goodbye?

He could also just be bored, stuck in this tent, miles away from civilization...

Will pulls back, and I feel the loss instantly, even as he gently caresses my cheekbones with his thumbs. "Cameron?"

I blink and look at him, seeing nothing but vulnerability and desire in his eyes.

"Will you kiss me back?" His voice is a plea, mirroring what I've been feeling all along.

I surge forward and practically climb onto his lap as I return his kiss, holding onto him just as desperately as he does to me, clinging to his shoulders and chest as our mouths move together.

Everything about him is familiar, but these movements between us, this feeling and this touching, are not.

I've dreamed about this moment for so long, and it's even better than I imagined.

I don't ever want it to end.

FIFTEEN

I wake up feeling all sorts of wonderful.

Until I open my eyes and realize I'm alone, tangled up in the mess of sleeping bags, and slightly delirious.

Will and I didn't stop kissing until the rain petered off and the pull of sleep became too strong. In his arms, I fell into a dreamless but much needed rest.

I sit up and stretch my muscles that are tight from all the exertion yesterday.

It is strange, though, that I can still have the same legs and arms and body I did twelve hours ago because I feel so different inside.

My clothing is half-dried, as I predicted, and I decide instead of suffering through wearing damp clothing, I'll make do.

I reluctantly change into my spare Camp Creek shirt, then decide to remain in my polka dot sleep shorts. I'm just glad I packed an extra pair of socks to protect my feet from my damp tennis shoes.

After that, I repack the leftover food and my belongings, then roll up the sleeping bags, effectively bursting the bubble Will and I created in this little tent last night.

I take a breath, uncertain of what I'll find when I step outside, then pass through the flap of the tent.

The campers are all bleary-eyed and subdued, seemingly in no mood to expend unnecessary energy by talking. Some meander over toward the beached kayaks while others sit around what would have been an excellent fire pit, had the rain not been an issue.

Will glances up from organizing the now-dismantled boys' tent as I approach him.

"Hey," I say a little tentatively.

He waves to me, holding one of the poles. "Hey. How are you?"

"I'm good," I tell him evenly, trying to feel him out before I let out too much excitement.

A small smile spreads on his face as he takes in my somewhat disheveled appearance.

"Will, are we heading out soon?" one of the campers whines.

Another girl pipes up. "Yeah, can we? This is boring."

"As soon as the stuff is ready," Will says to them.

I close the distance, moving to hold open the bag for him to shove the remaining pieces of the dismantled housing into. With that, our campsite—minus the tent I just vacated—is ready to go, so Will and I work silently in tandem as we finish packing up the rest.

I'm always conscious of myself, and of him, in his presence, and this morning, I think we're a bit softer, gentler maybe, around each other.

We're still the same people, of course, but something has shifted.

I don't have proof, but I can *feel* it.

But now's not the time to bring it up.

Will secures the final tie on the kayak he'll tow back down the river.

"We should head out," he announces to me and the campers in our proximity. "The water will probably be a little rough today, so we need to be extra careful."

"Okay," I tell him, sliding my backpack on my shoulders and over my life vest.

Will expertly gets into his kayak, then starts out in the lead, paddling in front of the group to double-check it's safe to proceed.

I hang back to ensure no one gets left behind, but in reality, it might be me who holds up the rest of the group.

Each stroke forward feels like my muscles are being ripped open.

It takes us hours of maneuvering through the slightly choppy waters to reach a spot we can stop at for a lunch of, regrettably, more peanut butter sandwiches. For dessert, I dump the rest of the Skittles in my mouth, knowing I'll need the sugar to help me power through the remainder of the afternoon.

We get underway again, and I try to keep my mind occupied with thoughts of Will, whose muscular form I can see if I squint, and just how beautiful it is out here.

I don't think I'll be going on any overnight camping trips anytime soon, but I suppose there is something magical about waking up in nature.

Plus, after last night's weather, everything is more brilliant, green, and lush, and it doesn't take an artist's eye to appreciate it.

Still, I nearly weep with relief when I see the van, waiting for us just where we left it.

We load up the kayaks in the trailer—a group effort, as we're all spent—then practically collapse into our seats as we buckle in. Now that I'm out of the water, a hot shower is the focus of my attention, but it doesn't come quickly.

The return trip takes almost twice as long as when we first came this way. The rain washed out a few of the main roads, which means I have to navigate us around with spotty cell service and an old-school map I found in the glove compartment.

By the time we drive through Camp Creek's gates, I'm exhausted, mentally and physically, and I want nothing more than to get cleaned up and devour the biggest dinner Bellamy will serve me.

Well, that's not true.

Because as I drag myself out of the passenger side, I watch Will interact with some campers—and nothing makes my heart more full than seeing him smile and just be himself.

"Don't neglect properly caring for these just because you're tired, okay?" Will says pointedly.

"Okay," the campers chorus back.

He shakes his head as they all drag their kayaks down the hill toward the water. "I swear, it's a miracle that Camp Creek manages to survive each summer."

I frown as I notice he's favoring his good leg. "Do you need help?" I ask.

"No," he says quickly before sighing and leaning against

the side of the van. "I can take care of this. Or have one of my assistants do it."

"Okay," I say.

He glances at his phone, checking the time. "Dinner should be starting soon."

"I know. I'm going to grab something quick, then go shower."

"Me, too, in a bit," he says.

I tuck my hair behind my ears, giving myself a second to pull my guard up. "Would you meet me in the art cabin after? We should...probably talk about last night."

As much as I wish he would give me *something* to work with, Will betrays nothing on his features as he nods.

"Sure," he says evenly.

I offer him a tight smile before I set off toward the mess hall.

Bellamy is nowhere to be found when I approach the counter, so I have to coax one of the other workers into giving me a portion before anyone else arrives.

And although it's just a plate of chicken tenders and fries, I swear it's the best meal I've had in weeks.

After I've consumed a sufficient number of non-sugary calories, I head back to Tori's and my cabin to wash off the river water and rain.

I'm relieved she's not here to pepper me with questions and press for details, leaving me alone to process my thoughts and ready myself for what tonight will bring.

Or, at least, what I *hope* it will bring.

The end goal, in my mind, is to have a straightforward conversation about last night and what it meant to him and then go from there.

I need to know if it was a fluke or some sort of bubbling over of feelings he's suppressed over the years, and I'm trying to not get too excited as I fixate on the latter.

I want answers, and I want an explanation.

But most of all, I want him.

I dress carefully, picking the best underwear and bra I brought with me to pump myself up, and it's a good break from the everyday stuff I usually go through. I slide on my jean shorts, Radiohead shirt, and sandals, then double-check my hair and makeup in the mirror before I head out.

Will's already at the art cabin when I arrive, arms crossed on his chest as he leans against the counter.

I admire him briefly, oddly enjoying how his hair is damp and messy from his shower, as he studies some of my pieces on display, then let the door slam shut behind me to signal my arrival.

I stutter-step forward, unsure what kind of greeting is now appropriate.

Because Will's right.

Things *are* different now.

I knew this summer would bring change and sadness while trying to say goodbye to a place I love as the inevitable future approaches.

Part of me dreamed of declarations of long-held feelings, along with reassurances and fiery passion. But all I can do is stand awkwardly, trying to remember what the hell I planned on saying to him once we were finally alone again.

"Hey," I manage.

Will crosses the room and pulls me into his arms for a hug, and I easily fold into his embrace.

I give into the gesture so wholly that if it were possible, I'd melt into him completely.

I breathe in the light and familiar scent of the Moreno laundry detergent, along with the sandalwood smell of the body wash he and Bellamy share, clinging to that comfort as I rest my head against his chest, right where his ink is hidden beneath the layer of his shirt.

"I still can't believe you have a tattoo," I murmur.

I can feel the rumble of laughter in his chest.

"Something to always remember you by," he says quietly.

I pull back, keeping my hands on his sides, and quirk a brow. "Are you being ominous on purpose?"

He shrugs as he releases me, moving back—with a slight wobble in his walk—to the counter.

I don't ask how he's feeling because I know it will immediately create walls between us that I don't want to rebuild.

Instead, I muster up every ounce of direct courage I have within me and let it spill. "I want to talk about last night."

Will runs a hand through his hair, slightly obscuring his face. "I'm not sure what to say."

"Last night was incredible," I say. "And it's something I would very much like to do again."

He sinks his teeth into his bottom lip, a move I know is the result of him not agreeing with me but trying to figure out how to say it.

I shake my head in irritation. "Why are you pushing against this? Before last night, I thought you didn't have any feelings for me, and that's why you shut me down originally."

"I just don't think it's a good idea. I...agree with what you said that we should just be friends."

And that infuriates me.

Because there was absolutely nothing *friendly* about what we were doing last night.

I laugh sardonically. "You're either in complete denial or you're lying to me, and I don't know what's worse."

He smiles sadly. "Cameron, I've known you for as long as I can remember. You're a part of me and Bellamy and my whole life. And we've barely even lived."

"I'm not following," I say warily.

"I don't want this for you."

I narrow my eyes. "*This*? What does that even mean?"

"You're going to go off to school in the fall," Will continues. "You're going to meet so many people and learn and grow, and so am I. We're going to grow apart, and I refuse to complicate things. I can't be a distraction for you, Cameron. I can't drag you down just because you feel tied to me out of guilt."

I open my mouth to argue but stop as I process what he's saying. "You think I want to be with you because I feel *guilty*? What, over the accident?"

He shifts, crossing his arms in front of his chest, and clenches his jaw. "I know you do. Every single time you look at me, you get a reminder of it. The blood. The screaming. The hospital. The recovery. I want you to be able to look at someone without wondering if they're okay."

I understand why he's gotten that impression.

But it's not totally true.

"Will," I start, throat thick. "I don't look at you with remorse or pity or any of those things. I look at you like you're everything to me. Because you are."

"You feel that way now, Cameron, but we have so much life left to live. We're barely a third of—"

"A fifth," I chime in.

Even with the tension between us, he still gives me an amused look. "What?"

"Bellamy and I made a pact that we'd live until we were at least one hundred."

Will lets out a breath. "Even worse. You're ready to make all of these decisions now, but—"

I huff and brush past him, which clearly surprises him.

Telling him isn't enough to make him understand, so I need to show him.

Wordlessly, I squeeze a massive dollop of black paint onto a palette, then eye one of my more recent pieces.

It's sort of an abstract take on the mountains and water, but it all started with that little curved line in the shape of his scar, the basis for all my art.

"Cameron," Will gasps as I raise the brush to the canvas. "What are you doing? Don't ruin your work because you're mad at me."

"I'm not ruining it," I tell him evenly. "And I'm not mad. I'm proving a point."

I smear the black paint down, my movement controlled but somewhat brutal, then go on to my next piece.

It's my most traditional image, just flowers in a small vase, similar to the one I saw on Rebecca's desk the other week. Even though the stems are mostly straight and narrow, I began with the edge of a shadow on the glass, and that's what I highlight now.

I repeat the motions in the loudest silence I've ever been subjected to, and after the fifth time I emphasize Will's definitive mark in my pieces, I drop my brush and turn to him.

"Don't you see?" I implore, taking in his narrowed eyes and closed-off posture. "There is no you holding me back. There is only you in everything."

He doesn't move as I reach for him.

I press my palms on his chest, and with the heat of my hands, I will the tension to leave his body.

"Cameron," he says quietly. "I...thought you knew. That I have *always* loved you. I just...wanted something better for you."

Those words stop me in my tracks.

Will loves me.

And he just admitted it so calmly and matter-of-factly that it's almost infuriating how he's able to say it so plainly, curtailed in his own insecurities.

No, it's not *almost* infuriating.

It just *is*.

"What if you just pushed all of that aside? What if you disregarded all of those thoughts where you think you aren't deserving or you're trying to protect me in your own convoluted way, and I let go of the fact that you've let me spend the last year with a wounded heart?" I straighten up, glad to be eye to eye with him as he remains slumped against the counter. "What if you just let me love you?"

He exhales and softens a bit.

Encouraged by this, I wrap my arms around his neck,

silently begging him to lower his mouth to mine and give in.

"I'm scared," he admits quietly, placing his hands on my waist to keep me fixed.

"Of what?" I ask quietly. "It's just me and you."

"That's just it, Cameron. It's not just you, like you're some random girl. You're *you*, my forever dream girl." He pauses, closing his eyes. "I had nightmares for months after the accident. In them, I somehow managed to hurt you even worse, and every time I woke, I promised myself I would never, ever do anything like that to you again."

"You've broken that promise already," I admit with a frown. "This last year has been painful, Will."

"But I thought you'd moved on," Will argues. "First with Mike, then with Dave."

"Dan, you mean?" I can't help but smirk.

"Whatever," he says dismissively.

I tug the ends of my hair in frustration. "I only tried to do so because of you. I thought you didn't want to be with me, not that you were just being stubborn. You *told* me you weren't interested."

"Well, let me *show* you that I am."

After awarding me with a challenging look, he finally kisses me.

It's not the slow, tentative, exploratory movement of last night—it's urgent and uninhibited and everything I want and need at this very moment.

He pulls at my hips, then swaps our positions, pushing me up to sit on the edge of the counter.

I wrap my legs around his waist, wishing he was even

closer, and when he leans into me, I can't help but revel in his all-consuming presence.

I move my hands down his chest, then slip them up beneath his shirt to feel him, somewhat in shock that I'm invited to do such a thing.

As I explore him, his hands tangle in my hair, and his lips move to my neck, leaving a trail of kisses in his wake. Just as I let out a sigh of contentment, the cabin door swings open, hitting the wall beside it with a slam.

We jolt and whip around to face our intruder, both of us flushed, breathless, and likely looking a little guilty. In our position, there's absolutely no pretending we weren't just doing the things we were.

I groan at the two people standing at the entrance, deciding that I would have rather been discovered by anyone—even Rebecca and Matthew—than these two.

Because I doubt I'll ever live this down.

"Someone had a productive kayak trip," Tori says smugly, crossing her arms on her chest.

Bellamy gives us a devilish smile. "What are you two doing in here?"

"What are *you* doing here?" I retort, letting go of my hold on Will to stand on my own two feet.

Tori and Bellamy exchange a glance before looking guiltily back at me.

"The same as us, I think," Will offers with a chuckle.

It's then I notice the picnic basket in Bellamy's hand and the slightly pink tinge to his cheeks.

I gasp in disbelief as understanding hits me. "You've been using the art cabin as your hookup spot?"

"Well, it didn't even occur to me to do so until I came

looking for you one day and found Brody and Caitlin in a very interesting position…"

"Oh my god," I say, instantly recoiling. "Is everyone using this place to fool around in? I work with *children* on their *art* here, and now it's all defiled."

Tori rolls her eyes. "Relax, Cameron."

"How can I possibly relax while processing this information?" I say incredulously.

My roommate simply snorts and turns her focus to the art pieces on display around the room.

"Ah," Tori says knowingly, apparently noticing the recent brushstrokes. "So, Will has finally discovered his place in all of your work?"

Will turns to me, looking more shocked than accusatory. "All of it?"

"Yes," Tori vocalizes for me. "Even her little doodles."

Bellamy sets the basket on the counter and reaches over to pat his brother on the back. "It's the starting point to everything she does. You're an idiot for not realizing it sooner."

Will reaches for my hand, squeezing it before he brings it up to his chest. "I can't help but agree."

SIXTEEN

I shield my eyes from the sun as I watch Will fiddle with the second sail.

Yesterday, I covered all the seams and new scraps of fabric in paint, making the lines look dramatic and violent instead of simply sewn together, and they look pretty good now that they're strung up.

In the week since we've become *official*, we've spent nearly every spare second together working on the sailboat. I've had a flood of inspiration, and he's been motivated to finish it up before our last days here, so it's worked out well.

And finally, after stealing an hour here and there—and mixing in kissing, laughing, and a little bit of touching—it's ready for its first voyage.

"You really think this is going to win you that internship?" Tori asks from her place beside me on the beach.

"I hope so," I tell her.

"A big risk for something so important," she muses.

I eye her skeptically, wondering if she isn't a fan of this entire endeavor. "I thought about submitting some pieces from my sketchbook, but this is more unique. Besides, my art teacher said my painting skills are better than my drawing ones."

Tori wrinkles her nose. "Your teacher is full of shit."

"Well, you do have decades of expertise criticizing art," I say with a laugh.

"I don't need any to tell you that your work with charcoal results in some of the most beautiful creations I've ever seen." She flips her hair over her shoulder in an exaggerated gesture. "And trust me, I know beauty."

"You do," I agree with a smile. "But I think this is great."

She shrugs, giving the boat another scan. "Whatever. Consider my curiosity tickled, though."

I frown at her lack of enthusiasm but try not to let it bother me because I've spent hours and hours on this project, and I have a lot riding on the success of it.

"It's *green*," Eden nearly screams as her little legs rapidly carry her toward us.

Will laughs at her excitement. "It is. The perfect shade of green."

I nod in confirmation at Eden's wide eyes. "Yes."

"It *is* perfect," she says, standing in awe.

The shade ultimately is something between Hunter Green and Emerald Green, according to the paint swatches I've compared it with. It's earthy but still a little shiny, the perfect balance of both.

"I'm glad you think so," I say with a smile. "Because I've decided to name it Eden Green, if that's okay with you."

She blinks up at me. "Really?"

"Really," Will confirms. "Do you want to come along for the inaugural ride?"

"Inaugural means first," I quickly define for her.

"I know what it means," she says flippantly. "And...I guess."

"Then go ahead and get yourself a life vest," Will tells her, pointing to the storage shack a few feet away.

"So, what's the plan?" Bellamy asks. "You want me to take pictures of you on the boat while it's in the water?"

I nod. "I've got a few closeups from here, but I can only imagine how the whole thing will look once the wind is blowing in the sail and the gleam of the setting sun is reflecting on it."

Bellamy gives a mocking sigh. "So poetic."

I merely scowl at him.

"I'm ready!" Eden says, buckling her life vest as she rejoins us.

Will holds out his hand. "Here, I'll help you up."

She reaches for him, trying to avoid getting her shoes wet in the low tide, then clambers onboard.

I follow right after.

"Are *you* ready?" Will asks me, holding onto the edge of the hull.

I grab the two ropes that he has given me hours of instruction on using, then beam at him. "Definitely."

He hops out to give the boat a good push before he

jumps back in, and the craft rocks slightly as it adjusts to his weight.

I expected a big rush of wind and a burst of movement, but we merely float.

"Should I wait for the wind?" Bellamy calls from the shore.

"Let me see if I can help," I yell back.

The sail is extended, but being empty of air, it looks kind of droopy and sad, so I tug on it, trying to make something, anything happen.

But it's fruitless.

"Maybe once we get in the middle of the lake, it will pick up," Will offers, one hand on the tiller to steer us that way. "Remember what you learned about steering a sailboat, Eden?"

"If you ever need to get away, just 'turn toward trouble,'" she says proudly.

"Good," Will praises. "Do you want to try it?"

She shakes her head, looking a little uneasy in her seat between us.

"Are you okay?" I ask her as we start to pick up speed.

She nods but keeps her hands folded on her lap. "I'm fine."

I don't believe her, but I don't push it, allowing myself to sit back and appreciate the ride.

I love the view of Camp Creek from this distance.

It's peaceful, and even though it's not exactly what I pictured—speeding across the lake with a massive wake and whipping winds—I think it will work.

Will reaches over and squeezes my hand, likely similarly appreciating our surroundings.

I'll definitely miss this view next summer and all the ones that follow. Maybe I can come back to visit and see how much the trees have grown and keep track of what other additions have been made to the camp. I hold onto that thought as we continue sailing.

Once we hit the middle of the lake, the deepest part, that's about one hundred yards from the beach, we idle.

"I should have brought my phone," I say, a little annoyed with myself. "I just hope Bellamy's getting some good shots."

"No!" Eden suddenly gasps, lifting her feet up off the deck as she leans back in her seat.

I turn toward her to see the issue, only to feel wetness seeping into my own socks.

"Will," I say frantically, gesturing to the widening hole at our feet.

What must have started as a puncture is rapidly crumbling into the size of an apple, encouraging lake water to join us aboard.

I cup water in my hands and toss it over the side, but it's laughable how ineffective my effort is.

"Oh, no, no, no, no," Eden says, gripping her life vest.

Will springs into action, grabbing the toolbox underneath the bench seat before scrambling over to us. He tears off a piece of duct tape with his teeth, trying to plug the area he swore he repaired weeks ago.

But, of course, it doesn't work.

"Do you think if we can turn around we'll be able to make it to shore?" I ask him.

"We can try," Will says.

We both lean over, putting a hand in the water and

paddle, but it doesn't help one bit. We seem to realize at the same moment that we've drifted too far away to make it back before the boat goes under.

"Abandon ship?" Will asks with a grimace as the water level moves quickly up my calves.

"What?" Eden yells, nervously eyeing the deepest part of the lake. "We have to swim back?"

"It'll be fine," I assure her.

"Cameron," she says, eyes wide. "I can't swim, remember?"

"I remember, but you have your life vest on, and Will and I are right by your side."

"And I'll even go first," he offers.

She doesn't look at all reassured.

He jumps in and starts treading water, then holds up his hand.

Eden looks at him doubtfully. "I don't think I can do it."

"You can," I encourage.

I don't mention that, soon enough, she's not going to have a choice.

"Here," I say, holding out my hand for her to take. "Hold onto me while you reach for Will."

"Come on," Will adds brightly, paddling backward toward the shore. "I've got you."

Eden looks terrified as the boat officially begins to sink.

"It's okay," I tell her. "Jump in three, two, *one*."

I can't tell if she leaps or I throw her, but she lands with a splash beside Will, who immediately grabs onto the back of her life vest as she wraps her arms around him.

I give the boat one last frown before I fall into the water, moving at my own pace a few feet behind them.

Will double-checks to make sure that I'm following because he, of course, is much faster than me.

"Go ahead," I urge, eyes locked on Eden, who thankfully doesn't look too shaken by the ordeal.

In fact, as I swim behind them, I don't see signs of panic on her features, just wide eyes, like she can't decide if she wants to burst out in tears or laugh like a maniac.

I let out a breath of relief as they hit the shore, and Tori pulls a slightly sputtering Eden into her arms.

Moments later, I crawl onto the beach and collapse.

"Are you okay?" Will asks, still catching his breath.

"Yes," I promise as I undo my life vest. "Eden, are you okay?"

"Yes," she says, still clinging to Tori.

"I got a few pictures," Bellamy says with a wince as he offers me my phone back.

"Right," I say, flipping through the semi-blurry photos that look embarrassingly juvenile.

"And he also took a video of the ship going down," Tori adds. "It's pretty epic."

"What a disaster." I sigh at them, then take in Will's frown. "And, oh my gosh, Will, I'm so sorry about the boat."

"It's fine," he says genuinely. "Really. I'm more upset about this for you than for me."

I run my hands through my hair. "But it's gone, and you put so much work into it."

Will reaches over to squeeze my hand. "Cameron, it's all right. I'm okay with it."

"What are we going to tell Rebecca and Matthew?" I

continue, on the brink of a breakdown. "And my submission, what the hell am I going to do?"

"Don't do this," Bellamy says, kneeling down beside me. "We'll fix it all."

I sputter. "But—"

"Tell me why you like art," Bellamy interjects.

"What?" I balk.

"Do it. Tell me. Now."

I take a deep breath and latch onto the sight of his serene expression as I exhale, trying to follow his instructions.

"You know why," I say quietly, heart slowly going back to normal.

"Tell me again."

I close my eyes briefly before fixing my gaze between Bellamy and Will, who I catch sharing a look of concern. "Art is like finding the perfect song to match the moment, only I get to capture it and make the feeling permanent."

"And did that project encapsulate that feeling?" Tori jumps in.

I consider it for a minute. "No."

"So, what will?" Will asks me.

I turn to face him full-on, taking in the slight flush of his face and the gentleness in his eyes, and my fingers twitch to trace all the little lines of texture in his skin.

And I have my answer.

"Let's get cleaned up, and then you can come by mine and Tori's place," I tell him.

"Of course," he agrees immediately.

Tori squeezes Eden's shoulders. "We'll walk you back to your cabin, okay?"

"And Bellamy?" I call before the trio leaves my sight.

"Yeah?"

"The art cabin is yours for the night."

He looks at Tori, and they share a wicked smile.

SEVENTEEN

I don't have much to set the mood—just my two camp-issued, white pillows, the quilt I brought from home, and a few battery-operated flashlights.

But as I think about the perfect setting for this, I can't think of anything better.

I can smell the water, even from hundreds of feet away, along with pine and the campfire one of the cabins just lit in the distance.

"What's all this?" Will asks as he lets himself in.

"I'm finally going to get you to sit for a portrait," I announce.

He flinches, then lets out a sigh of surrender. "Okay."

"I know you don't like the attention, but this is all I've got. I'm out of ideas."

"No, it's fine," he reassures me. "I'm happy to help. Just tell me what I need to do."

I can't help but smile as I gesture to the bed. "Get comfortable."

He kicks off his shoes before he sits, then fluffs the pillows and lies back.

I join him, sitting cross-legged at the end of the bed to get a view of him straight-on. "Can you brush your hair away?" I ask gently.

Without hesitating, he keeps his eyes on mine as he lifts his hand to move the rogue lock of hair over the side of his face.

I can't help but fall even more in love with him at his willingness to be so vulnerable for me.

"This feels very *Titanic*, you know," he says lightly.

I chuckle. "I haven't asked you to pose nude."

Will shuffles a bit, adjusting his posture to get more snug. "And, worse, you haven't offered me a massive diamond necklace."

"Not yet," I say, which makes him laugh. "Okay, now, can you try to stay somewhat still?"

"Can I breathe?" he asks playfully.

"I hope so." I pick up a piece of charcoal and my sketch-book. "Stop distracting me. I need to focus."

The corner of his mouth ticks up. "So demanding."

I give him a mock-glare, then I begin, fully aware that he's scrutinizing me as intently as I am him.

Drawing Will feels more intimate than anything else we've done so far—not just the physical stuff, the kissing and the touches, but the truths we've exchanged.

Not one single part of our body touches at this moment, but I feel a connection to him, the same one I've always felt was missing with everyone else.

I start with the scar, of course.

That single line is so deeply embedded in my memory, I

don't even have to look at him as my hand moves...but I do.

Just because I can.

Slowly, that one stroke becomes the crest of a mountain. It's not one of the several on the edge of camp or any that we passed on the river or dirty roads. It's the movement of our lives together, swooping up and getting a little bumpy before leveling out and becoming perfectly even to fade up into the rest of him.

I do the eyes next, the sun and the moon. I capture the midday rays that peek through the clouds that have poured far too much rain for my liking and reflect off the lake. The planet illuminates the darkness, a beacon of light and hope that cuts through the treetops.

His hard jaw becomes a river, framing everything else, and I capture the soft curve of his lips just above it, making them the basin, the outlet for the things he keeps inside.

The nose and eyebrows are next, two features that define him just as much as everything else. I add flowers and stars and little wisps of grass, all the good things in the world that deserve prominence, too.

I stare at the real live version of him, knowing that I'll never get tired of doing so, as my hand moves effortlessly over the page.

I create our world within his features—one free of all trauma, pain, and self-doubt.

Because being with him, and capturing him this way, I think I could make anything happen.

The sun has firmly set by the time I've finished the drawing and am pulled out of my creative frenzy, and I take a minute to assess my work on the page.

It's half-portrait, half-abstract, but it's him.

"Can I see it?" Will asks quietly, breaking my trance.

I've never been shy about showing him or Bellamy my artwork, but this feels different, like I'm handing over a piece of my soul depicted through smudges on paper.

When I nod my permission, he sits up and reaches for the sketchbook, holding it like it's precious as he takes in the image on the page.

The look on his face is one I've seen him wear many times over the years.

I can associate it now with him trying to untangle ropes by the water or solve a math problem at school—it's like he knows the answer is right in front of him, but he can't quite figure it out.

He offers the portrait back to me, almost reluctantly, then I lean over to set it on Tori's bedspread.

"Is that how you see me?" Will asks, reaching for my hand.

The low tone of his voice is intense.

I'm hoping it stems from some deep-rooted emotion I've tapped into rather than pain or disgust.

As I search his eyes, I notice that same lock of hair has fallen over his face again, but I don't reach for it, letting him have that little bit of a shield if he needs it.

"Yes," I admit, forcing the words through my throat. "It is."

His thumb traces the lines of my palm.

Will has done this gesture before, just once that I can recall—as if I'd ever forget any moment between us—and it's soothing.

The first time, we were at a funeral for my grandmother,

who died from natural causes after a long and happy life when I was seven. I didn't feel any sadness or remorse at the time, being too young to really understand what was going on.

But I remembered the way Will's hand felt in mine, his gentleness causing my heart to pound and my body to feel like it was fidgeting, even though I wasn't actually moving.

I returned that gentle touch years later as he and I sat side by side at the kitchen table when Bellamy came out to his parents, providing a united front for whatever their reaction would be. The focus was on his brother that day, of course, but still, I hoped my grasp brought Will the same comfort that he gave me.

It's easy to recall so many memories with him—all the pivotal stuff and the little things that are equally important.

Because they're all ours.

I love that we've gotten to share so much time, experiencing a lifetime of happiness, pain, exhilaration, growth, embarrassment, and a whole range of emotions before we've even really figured out who we are as people.

But that's where Will and I have differed.

I've looked at him with the hope he'll be my future, and he's been thinking that I'll just be part of his past.

"I just wish..." He trails off and sighs.

I squeeze his hand. "Yeah?"

"I just wish that I could show you how I feel about you, like you've done for me."

I remove one of my hands from his to place my palm on his chest. "You've already permanently marked yourself, Will."

He shakes his head, frustrated, like he thinks tattooing

his skin somehow means less than a portrait that took me a few hours to create.

I lean forward and press a gentle kiss on his lips.

It's still a little nerve-wracking and wonderful and thrilling that I get to do this now, but there's no better way to cement this moment in my mind.

He pulls back after a minute, a little breathless.

"Cameron," he whispers.

"Will," I say, feigning exasperation. "What am I going to do with you?"

But he's not teasing me.

His expression is far from light, and there's a crease on his forehead, and his eyes are a little dark and narrow as he runs his thumb along my bottom lip.

I try to catalog his expression, recall if I've seen it before, and the answer is no. I haven't, and that's as terrifying as it is exhilarating.

"Do you know how much I love you?" Will rasps before pressing a kiss on the base of my throat.

"I don't," I admit quietly.

My eyes flutter shut as he slides a hand up under the hem of my shirt. I gasp at the warmth of his fingers on my skin, delighting in all the new feelings and emotions he's bringing out of me.

He pulls on my hips, gently but firmly, to guide me over to him.

As he moves to lie down, I startle in realization at what he's intending to start.

"We don't have to do this," I say, pulling back. "I mean, I want to. I've thought about it for so long, but you don't have to prove anything to me. I know—"

"Cameron," he interrupts, moving closer to me. "I *want* to do this with you. All of it. Everything. You and me."

I swallow. "Okay."

He fingers the ends of my hair, dropping his gaze, and I marvel that I've never seen him this uncertain and *nervous*.

"I might not be good at it," he admits, a blush working its way up his neck.

I give my best smile as I settle down beside him and drop a hand on his chest. "Not possible."

He kisses me again, picking up right where we left off.

I tuck his hair behind his ears, not letting him hide anything from me.

As nervous hands remove articles of clothing, I lose myself in him, reveling in the newness and exploration until we're bared to each other in a way I never thought possible.

"Let me love you," he whispers.

And so I do.

EIGHTEEN

I dip the tip of my brush into the Eden Green paint for the final time, then smear my tiny "C" signature in the bottom right corner.

I could have just scribbled it with pencil, but I like the way the paint contrasts with the black and white.

A few days ago, I added little dots and highlights of green over the charcoal, and today, I finally feel ready to send this off.

It's fitting that, on the last day of camp, I'm putting the finishing touches on the portrait that is the culmination of this time Will and I have shared—and that it coincides with when we are looking ahead to our future.

As I leave the art cabin and head up toward the main office, I blow on my painted name, drying it quickly as I mentally prepare to send in my submission.

I bound up the steps, push the creaky screen door open with my elbow, then scan the room for office supplies that I know Bellamy has pilfered before.

And I stop short at the sight of a familiar face.

"Hi, Rebecca," I say as I approach where she's seated behind a desk.

"Yes?" She glances up from some papers she's perusing to smile at me. "Oh, hi, Cameron. Everything okay?"

"Yeah, but I was wondering if you happen to have an envelope that will fit this size?" I ask as I hold up my portrait of Will.

It's funny how carelessly I show it off to her now when it's probably my most prized possession—I'm almost reluctant to ship it off.

Her eyes widen as she stands. "Oh my gosh. This is fantastic."

"Thank you."

Rebecca comes around from behind the desk to get a better look, holding her folded hands to her chest as she takes in my drawing. "May I?"

I nod, then hold it out for her to take.

She grips the paper at the edges to bring it closer to her face. "The detail, the line work, the shading...all of it is gorgeous. I think I have some wrapping that will keep this safe."

Before I can utter more words of gratitude, she opens one of her many cabinets, pulling out bubble wrap, brown paper packing material, and an unassembled box. Oddly enough, she then opens a drawer filled with kitchen supplies, including dishware and plastic wrap.

She pulls out a small, rectangular box of something, but I can't see the name on the package.

"What is that?" I ask her curiously.

"Baking paper," she says.

I tilt my head. "For what?"

"It'll protect the charcoal from smudging. Did you use any setting spray on the piece?"

"No," I admit. "I was just going to toss it in an envelope and let it go."

"What?" Rebecca looks at me like I'm genuinely insane. "But it's *art*, Cameron! You need to take care of it."

"I guess you're right," I admit with surprise.

I try to help her wrap the piece and get it ready for shipping, but she insists on doing it herself, apparently afraid that I'm going to ruin my own work.

I find that amusing rather than invasive.

"Who's this off to?" she asks after placing the final piece of packing tape on the box.

I pull up the name and address on my phone. "The Yarra DeLinch Gallery in Pittsburgh."

She blinks in surprise. "Are you submitting this piece to put on exhibit?"

I shake my head. "I'm trying to get an internship with the artist in residence."

Rebecca hands me a marker to jot down the address on the front of the box, watching me carefully, and I shift awkwardly.

"That gallery is one of three owned by the Archer family," she says eventually. "I know Abigail, the owner and curator, from art school."

I don't know what surprises me more—that she has connections or that she went to art school herself.

"Wh-what?" I stutter.

She smiles slyly. "Who do you think painted the mural on the ceiling of the art cabin?"

My jaw drops. "Oh my gosh. You did? No way."

"Yes way," she says on a laugh. "I was in your role when I met Matthew many, many years ago. His dad owned this camp, but he was working as a counselor that year."

I try to think of the most tactful way to pry. "Did you...pursue art after that?"

"For a while. Then things got busy around here, and Matthew's dad got sick. It just ended up that we took over, and everything else fell to the wayside."

I simply nod, unsure what to say.

Because it occurs to me that the root of Will's hesitancy about us getting together was exactly that.

Not that I'd give up my passion for him in any way but that I might let his issues and self-doubt overshadow my drive and detract from my art.

I think I've done an admirable job of proving just how much I adore and need him.

"I know talent when I see it," Rebecca says, jarring me from my inner thoughts so I drop the smile I hadn't realized I'd formed.

"I really appreciate that," I tell her when I recover. "Your mural has been a huge source of inspiration for me this summer."

"That is very kind of you to say, but you know art is subjective. I wonder, then, if your reaction to my piece has been more about you finding yourself and your muse than anything else." She gives me a wink, then taps the box before moving it into the bin of outgoing mail. "I'll make sure this is sent out."

"Thank you so much. For this, and for everything here at Camp Creek over the years."

"Of course," she says, giving me a quick hug. "It's been an honor to have you here, Cameron. We will miss you very, very much."

I pull back and smile. "Does that mean I'm not allowed to come back to visit?"

"You're welcome here anytime." She pats my shoulder before she moves back to her desk. "But I think you have much more of the world to see, explore, and capture with your art."

"I hope so."

I give her a final wave before I let myself out.

I come across Brody and Caitlin, corralling lines of both cars and people in their attempt to get the campers all moved out and off the property.

I'm glad that my only duties are to do one last sweep of the art cabin, then figure out how to say goodbye to this place—and to Tori.

I head toward the mess hall, hoping that Will, Bellamy, and Tori will all be there.

As I walk, my phone vibrates in my pocket. I pull it out and frown because this is, like, the hundredth call from my sister since her visit to Camp Creek. I shake my head and hit ignore, as I always do, not wanting her to bring me down on my last day here.

I tuck my phone away and step inside, catching the sight of Bellamy sitting with Tori at our normal table, holding her hand and speaking softly.

Will sneaks up beside me and slides his arm around my

shoulders, letting his gaze follow mine. "Do you think they'll stay together?"

"I hope so," I say. "But I'm sure the statistic of relationships that start in high school and continue into college is abysmal."

"And we're already claiming a percentage of that number for us," Will says confidently, pulling me in for a kiss.

"I thought you said that Will isn't your boyfriend," Eden accuses sharply.

I can't help but chuckle as I release Will and turn to take in her furrowed brow. "He wasn't then, but he is now."

She eyes us warily. "Okay."

I bend down slightly to get on her level. "Are you leaving soon?"

"My mom is waiting for me, but I wanted to give you this before I go." Eden hands over a piece of scrap wood about the size of a sheet of paper.

The wood itself is painted in a base coat of white, and over top of it is depicted a shaky view of the scene outside the art cabin window.

There are a few stick figures, and even a sailboat in the water—floating properly, not mid-sink—all painted in the shade of Eden Green we created over the summer.

"This is amazing," I tell her, reaching out for a hug. "I love it."

"Good," she says, giving me a quick embrace.

"I've really enjoyed meeting you this summer, Eden."

I can't help but get a little emotional, moisture rapidly filling my eyes because I hate goodbyes.

"I'm going to miss you," I say, voice faltering.

And Eden, despite all the time we spent together this summer, manages not to waver.

"Bye," she says quietly, strong and defiant as always, then takes off.

I stand and watch her dash out of the mess hall, swallowing my sadness before it can fester into something more visible.

"She's something," Will says with a laugh.

"She is," I agree.

"And this is why I'm getting the hell out of here now," Tori says as she approaches us, gesturing to my misty expression.

Bellamy trails behind, looking like he's struggling to hold it together.

"Come on," she insists, holding out her arms. "One quick group hug, then I'm out."

I get to her first, wrapping my arms around her before I'm enveloped by the Moreno twins.

It's a nice, complete feeling, and I wonder if the four of us will be together again anytime soon.

"You all take care of yourselves, okay?" Tori says.

"Okay," I answer, my single word muffled against her shoulder.

"I expect big things from you, Cameron," she says seriously as she pulls back. "Will, don't be a stranger, and Bellamy...I'll see you soon, all right?"

He nods and crosses his arms over his chest.

Before Tori steps outside, she turns back and offers what I think is supposed to be her most motivational line yet.

"Just remember to shoot for the stars and try to land on the moon," she says proudly.

The emotional moment is broken by our laughter, and Tori offers us a wide smile before she departs.

All that's left is for Bellamy, Will, and me to give our hardest goodbye yet—to Camp Creek.

NINETEEN

"And how are my little lovebirds doing today?" Elena singsongs.

I stretch from where I lie on the couch, hitting my feet against Will's thigh and eliciting a smile from him.

"Fantastic," Bellamy answers on our behalf as he turns off the television. "We've just finished our rewatch of *The Office*."

Elena frowns in disapproval. "You all can't find some other way to occupy your time other than sitting in front of the television?"

Bellamy sighs. "I don't know what you want from us. We have a week left at home. Shouldn't you be thrilled that we're spending all this time here before we leave you?"

"Actually, Will and I have a date tonight," I announce.

It feels a little cringey to do so, but I know I'm cutting into a senseless argument that could absolutely go on for an hour—long enough for them to forget what they disagreed on originally.

"Lovely," Elena says genuinely.

Truth be told, I'd completely forgotten about having any sort of hesitation to bring a relationship between us into the dynamic of our families until we pulled into the driveway a week ago upon returning from Camp Creek.

I reached for Will's hand without thinking about it, only to be screamed at—happily—by Elena and my mother.

Suffice it to say, both sets of parents are overjoyed at our newfound connection, and they've actually been pretty respectful of not asking too many questions or teasing us about it.

Well, except for Elena, who pulled me aside last week to let me know that her wedding dress is still in storage, if the occasion arises for me to need it…

"I wish you were this enthusiastic about *my* dating life," Bellamy grumbles.

"With the soccer goddess, you mean?" Elena poses. "What's there to enthuse about? You texting her all day and staying up at night to FaceTime her? You're giving me nothing to work with!"

Will chuckles as his mother and brother argue back and forth.

My own mirth is interrupted when my phone pings with a notification.

I pull it out, expecting to just ignore a call from Piper or see a message from my future college roommate, but when my eyes land on the unread email, I gasp aloud.

"What is it?" Will asks, shifting closer to me.

"The internship," I say a little breathlessly as I click on the email.

My heart pounds as I speed-read the first few lines, then

I glance up, making eye contact with Will, then Bellamy and Elena.

"I got it!" I exclaim in shock.

The three of them yell and cheer, pulling me up for rounds of hugs and celebrations as they all gush with excitement and beg for details.

I join in, elated, and respond as best I can, but I'm almost suffering from whiplash at how everything has changed in the past few weeks.

"We should have a party tonight," Bellamy suggests. "A big, fancy dinner or something."

"Only if you want to," Will tells me. "We can catch the later show at the movies if you want to do both."

I smile. "Oh, I—"

A knock sounds at the front door, catching all of our attention.

"Who is that?" Bellamy asks.

Will rolls his eyes. "How am I supposed to know?"

I turn to Elena. "Are you expecting someone?"

"No," she says curiously.

We move toward the front entryway, and she unlocks the door and peeks out.

"Oh," she breathes, then takes a step back. "Piper."

I grimace at the sight of my sister, looking as polite and put-together as usual.

"Hello, Mrs. Moreno," she says. "May I come in?"

"Of course." Elena waves her inside. "Cameron is just behind me."

"Actually, I was hoping Bellamy would stick around, too. And Will, why not?" Piper smiles at us all but gets no reaction other than Elena's polite stepping out.

She clears her throat. "Cammie, I heard about the two of you, and I have to say, I'm so thrilled—"

"What do you want, Piper?" I ask, cutting straight to the point. "Aren't you supposed to be at school, living your fabulous life with your boyfriend?"

She blinks as her expression falls. "Right. That's why I'm here. I realized I needed to come and apologize in person."

"For what?" I scoff.

"For not realizing what a horrible sister I've been..."

I roll my eyes but don't open my mouth.

"...to the three of you."

That surprises me.

Given the way Will and Bellamy's eyes widen, it's a shock to them, too.

"Although we haven't always gotten along, you have been in my life forever, and I'm really ashamed that I didn't do more to support you." Piper stops and lets out a sigh. "I didn't realize the full extent of my failings until the whole family weekend thing with TJ, and I'm just really sorry."

We all remain silent, unsure how to respond.

She looks down at the ground and fidgets with her hands. "It took me all of five minutes in the car on the way home after visiting you to realize what an idiot I've been. And how awful he is."

"But you moved in with him," I press. "Mom said you got all moved into your new apartment the day we left Camp Creek."

She shakes her head. "I have my *own* apartment, a tiny studio right off campus. I love having my own space, and TJ...well, I'm pretty sure he's already moved on."

I don't pick up a shred of sadness in her voice, just maybe a little regret.

Bellamy clears his throat. "I appreciate the gesture, Piper, really I do. But driving four hours from the university just to apologize was totally unnecessary."

She shrugs. "I felt like I needed to clear the air before we randomly bump into each other on campus. Besides, I brought you something."

"You did?" Bellamy asks, curious.

A smile tugs at the corner of her mouth as she pulls out her phone. She shoots off a quick text, and then we all stand awkwardly and quietly in the foyer until the front door flings open again.

Tori bounds through it with a massive grin on her face. "Miss me?"

I laugh and pull her down for a hug, only for her to be practically ripped from my arms by Bellamy, who quickly wraps her in his.

"I missed you," she admits before planting a kiss on his mouth.

"I missed you, too," he tells her like he's totally relieved.

Tori gives him another peck before she turns to the rest of us. "So, what's been going on? Anything new and exciting?"

I grin. "Well…"

I repeat my news, and we go through the entire hug and celebration talk all over again.

It's not until later when both of our families are stuffed around the Moreno dining table eating *ropa vieja* that everything finally settles in.

Because this is not just a feel-good moment after the air has been cleared and a very sweet reunion has occurred. It's a general, warm, fuzzy feeling of contentment and appreciation of my surroundings.

I never thought I would feel that away from the view in the mountains, but it's taken me all this time to realize that, if I let myself, I can capture that feeling anywhere.

"What a summer we had," I murmur to Will.

He squeezes my hand. "What a life we have ahead."

TWENTY

TWO MONTHS LATER

College feels like its own version of summer camp.

I don't think I'm projecting just because I've traded the mountains, lake, and Bellamy's cooking for a life in the city.

But maybe I am.

Regardless, I'm still enjoying it immensely.

Thankfully, my roommate is great. She's less chatty but much cleaner than Tori, and I *almost* miss getting forced to do someone else's makeup and having to clear space by kicking socks to the other side of the room.

She is a fashion major, so when we're not commiserating over our common basic classes, she spends all her time sewing in her department's building.

And I'm busy, too, getting my art critiqued in class, studying for my general education tests, or soaking up as much information as I can at my internship.

But for now, I walk along the sidewalk, appreciating the rapidly cooling fall weather as I head to my destination.

As I eye the jutted-out entrance to the diner—which is modeled after a 1950s vibe with the staff in full costumes and on roller skates—my phone buzzes.

I pull it out and immediately smile at Bellamy's name.

Game night, his text reads, and it's accompanied by a ten-second video of Tori warming up on the field.

I angle my phone and take a selfie in front of the restaurant, then send *Date night!* back to him.

Bellamy's response is almost instant. *Love you. And that brother of mine.*

Lol. I'll pass along the message. Love you, too!

I smile as I slide my phone back into my purse, idling while I wait for Will.

He's usually the first one to arrive, but he had to stay after his night class today to ask his professor a question, so I get to people watch as I wait.

This is a new part of the city I've never been in, but Will heard good things about it from someone in his dorm, so we agreed to try it.

We've tried to stay true to our individual college experiences, making our own friends and finding a sense of community while still supporting each other.

But each week, we pick a night to spend together, just the two of us, and so today, it's a Wednesday night study date over breakfast for dinner.

It's no home-cooked meal by Bellamy, but it'll do just fine.

"Cameron," Will calls.

And still, after all this time, my heart flutters when our eyes meet.

As I look at him, I see the scar, the hair, the smile—he's the fixture of my life I can't imagine being without.

It's only him in everything.

Young Adult Romances

Everywhere, Always

Just Play Pretend

Only You in Everything

Perfect Little Flaws

The Extended Summer of Anna and Jeremy

The Stillness Before the Start

Adult Romances

In the Now

Nothing Personal for Breakfast

This Is Your Life

Young at Midnight

"The Islands of Anarchy" Series

New Wave

Rip Current

"The Royally Human Vampire" Series

Metallic Red

Yes, Your Majesty

FREE GIFT FOR YOU!

Want to make your book an autographed copy? Head over to Jennifer's website and get a free bookplate!

https://www.jenniferannshore.com/bookplate

CONNECT WITH JENNIFER

Hi there,

I cannot thank you enough for reading my work. Truly, it means the world to me!

I'd love to connect with you on social media if you're up for it. I'm on all the major social channels, including TikTok (@jenniferannshore) and Instagram (@shorely).

And don't forget to subscribe to my email newsletter (jenniferannshore.com/newsletter) for bonus scenes, new release announcements, giveaways, and more.

All my love! —Jennifer

ACKNOWLEDGMENTS

As one of those kids who went to summer camp every year growing up, I had a lot of fun reminiscing about the time and antics—and how nice it was to just have nothing to do but explore the outdoors and play around. While I definitely didn't have an experience like Cameron, I did have a lot of fun dreaming up and writing her story, and I need to thank the people who helped me with this book:

To begin, Jen McDonnell, you're truly magnificent, and I'm so grateful for our work together and our friendship.

Denise Leora Madre, you helped me change and shape this story for the better, and I can't thank you enough for your honesty, support, and comments that make me laugh out loud.

Dino Decespedes, thank you so much for your redirections and nudges on ensuring I properly represented a Cuban family. And for being genuinely cool and a person I admire!

Lindsay Hallowell, I love how I get to write this one before you read it so that you can correct my typos while I try to put into words how grateful I am for you! I truly appreciate you so very much.

Kelly Lipovich, thank you, once again, for using your incredible design chops to make this cover. I don't think I've ever told you this, but whenever I'm writing about a teen artist, I always think about that absurdly impressive painting you made in high school—the details are blurry to me now, but I remember being awed by your talent even then!

Emily Wright, you are such a gem, and I feel so lucky to have your thoughts and comments on my work. (And for our laughs!!!)

Birdtrek, I really appreciate your direction on Bellamy's character. He's a badass (just like you), and I'm so grateful for your time spent and notes on how to best support the trans community and accurately depict his journey.

Kilroy, my best friend and the best photographer in the world, thank you for your endless love and support—and for being my forever hypewoman.

And finally, to my readers and reviewers, I love you all so much. Thank you, thank you, thank you.

ABOUT THE AUTHOR

Jennifer Ann Shore is an award-winning, bestselling author based in Seattle, Washington.

She writes romance stories that go a little deeper than the standard tropes. Her lineup of more than a dozen books includes standalones, a dystopian series, and a vampire series—with titles such as "Perfect Little Flaws," "Young at Midnight," and "Metallic Red."

Prior to publishing, she led an impressive career in New York, first as a journalist and then as a marketing executive, gaining recognition for her work from companies such as Hearst and SIIA.

Be sure to sign up for her newsletter on her website (https://www.jenniferannshore.com) and follow her on Twitter (@JenniferAShore), Instagram (@shorely), and TikTok (@jenniferannshore).